Wine by the Glass

A collection of love tales by John D. Pitman

First published in Australia 2017 by Busybird Publishing

ISBN 978-1-925692-16-7

National Library of Australia Cataloguing-in-Publication entry:
Author: Pitman, John D., 1950-
Title: Wine by the Glass
ISBN: 978-1-925692-16-7

A CIP catalogue record for this book is available from the National Library of Australia.

Printed in Australia

From Roy to Cynthia

From the eternity of time we have but years
And from them we have snatched brief days.
Poor balm for hearts that always long to be
Together, with no parting of the ways.

A parting kiss. A tear that almost comes.
No, we are brave. Yet deep down inside
Is that hard gnawing pain that will not go
And there's a trembling lip that even we can't hide.

Yes, men may laugh, and sing and show brave face
While seen by others. Yet they are the same
As I am now. And will be forever
Whispering your name.

RAAF EX 50040 Corporal Roy Douglass Pitman 1943
(1917 – 1989)

(Published in Caress of the Moon, 1997)

Cynthia Pitman, 1919 - 2009

Contents

Grandma's Maid, Mary

Throughout our childhood, youth and much of our adolescence, my two sisters and I were rich, incredibly rich. We had loving grandparents whom we adored and who lived immediately across the road from us. Our grandmother, Lilian Mary Isobel Pitman, was my father's mother. Her maiden name was Bear, giving rise to her joke that we were descended from bears. Strangely, this family joke was one not shared with our schoolmates. She also had a brother Teddy, but that is another story.

Our grandmother was rich. She had a maid, Mary. Often we would be seated at Grandma's table.

'Cake for lunch? Oh, I don't think so, Mary says we've just run out, you'll have to eat the sandwiches. That includes the crusts, Jan.'

So we ate the sandwiches and were grateful for the Vegemite.

If our multi-talented grandmother was amazing, Mary was more so. She avoided chores like the plague.

'Could you put the kettle on please, dear? It's Mary's day off today, trust her to leave us in the lurch. No milk? Well, take my purse and slip up the street. If only Mary had been here.'

Childhood flatulence was poorly tolerated at Grandma's. Across the road, children could be seen and heard as often as wished, but preferably not smelt. Of Velvet soap, yes, fart, no.

On one occasion the rumblings of an over satiated bowel was vented loudly.

Grandma's runny nose wrinkled at the stench. 'Good Lord, was that thunder, Mary? Girls, bring in the washing immediately. Has someone got dog on their shoe? Now John, seeing you're closest, open the window. Quickly now, before we all asphyxiate. Be careful of the catch, it's wonky. Don't fall out. There's a good boy.'

For entertainment on wet days, it was a common occurrence in Croydon to go into Grandma's 'junk room.' Here, she kept a large cardboard box filled with clothes of all descriptions. Dressing up, we could act out our childhood fantasies: a queen addressing her subjects one minute or a policeman catching thieves the next. Her cosy wood-fired lounge easily became a ready-made stage that gradually deteriorated to resembling a bomb site by curtain call.

'Now children, Mary is out shopping. You'll have to clean up your own mess. Quickly now before she gets back. Everything back in the box and the box put away nicely. Thank you, girls.'

Playing charades and family get-togethers across the road were commonplace. Mary also loved fun but could not protect Grandma from over exuberance. At one gathering Grandma decided to demonstrate the Highland Fling. In a dramatic reel she flung herself around with true highland abandon only to crash heavily on the wooden floor. Mary was given six weeks off while Grandma stayed in hospital as her broken hip healed. Even on Grandma's return home we had to continue performing the maid's duties, emptying the potty secreted under her bed being the worst. This was yet another chore Mary refused to perform.

Mary the maid was a stickler for manners too. We had to sit 'nicely' and behave. After all, our parents were just across the road. Not that we were game to misbehave anyway - the 50's were a time of obedience towards adults.

'Oh dear! Has someone got their elbows on the table? Mary says that's very bad manners in the houses she's served in. Elbows off everyone,' and the old rickety table took on a new angle as we removed our elbows from the table. It was an unusual dining table, having the ability to tilt for compact storage. It also tilted on other occasions, which made for exciting meal times then and still does.

'Careful who sits on that chair,' she'd also warn, pointing. 'One of the legs is broken, the chair's not called Eileen for nothing.'

Grandma's nose often looked like a leaking tap so Mary had been called on to offer suggestions. Apparently she coined the expression 'Mrs Jones is at the door' to be inserted into conversation to warn Grandma of an imminent drip. Occasionally we kids, too polite to interrupt the adults talking, had to warn, 'too late, Mrs Jones is in the soup!'

Another expression Mary passed on through Grandma was 'FHB', standing for Family Hold Back. With her visitors often accepting hospitality at the last minute, meals took on a biblical aspect of feeding many with little. When 'FHB' was heard, everyone in the family within earshot was expected to take smaller portions. I wonder these days what the visitors thought of the strange sayings.

Come to think of it, Mary was not an efficient maid by modern standards. Requests for cleaning were met with such tardiness, it was easier for someone else to do it.

'Who knows where the vacuum cleaner is kept? Mary says she is too busy for vacuuming, we'll all have to chip in. Be careful of that rug and that the fringe doesn't end up down the tube again. My goodness, don't those windows look clean, we can see right across the road. You might like to remind your father, John, that my lawns are getting up a bit, so are yours, I note. Just the front, the back can last until next time.'

When Grandma's vast brass collection needed polishing, Mary would simply vanish. From the tin of Brasso, Cheryl's fingers would take on a blackened appearance in stark contrast to the brass's new golden gleam, for a while at least. There was no shortage of polishing, with brass Buddhas, brass monkeys, brass trays, brass candlesticks, brass everything in abundance. Hours flew by in pleasant activity.

It was obvious Mary's skills did not lie in cooking. She never left anything for us hungry kids to eat. So Grandma and her young assistants filled that void also. Tasty scones and cakes were 'whipped up' at a moment's notice, provided someone was willing to perform Mary's cleaning up duties afterwards. The old kitchen wood stove, almost always burning slowly, would be stirred into action, sending deliciously sweet aromas wafting down the hallway. Yummy. Our taste buds tingled, provided our tongues weren't burnt on the food, eaten as soon as it was pulled from the oven.

The maid, Mary, did not perform repairs either.

'Is that the bottom gone from your trousers again, John? Where's Mary when you want her? Well, slip them off and I'll patch them straight away. There's no one to see, stand near the fire if you're cold.' As Grandpa's printing press clanked away mechanically in the background, hands almost ceaselessly crocheting would miraculously transfer to needlework. With luck no one would visit at that time as the front door would have to be answered with us in just our underwear. Grandma was busy with the treadle sewing machine and Mary absent as usual.

Grandma's chip heater was an interesting device that Mary always forgot to light.

'Mary's simply developed amnesia lately. The water's gone cold again, she must have overlooked the heater. Could someone, preferably two of you, put a match to it? Be careful now and don't waste the kindling. Tell your father it's getting low again, and use only two briquettes, Money doesn't grow on trees, you know.'

Once, I proudly lit the chip heater by myself, the firebox filled to the brim with multiple briquettes. If two briquettes were good, surely more would be better, I reasoned. The heater fairly roared. Not long after, a heavy type of rain, unlike the usual acorns' noise, began to fall on the rusty tin roof from the overflow pipe.

'How many briquettes did you put in? No matter, I'll have hot water for a week now, but seeing Mary's indisposed at present, could you bring some more briquettes in from outside. There's a good lad. Mary's back plays up quite badly with heavy work.'

Grandma wasted nothing. Once raked up, all the leaves were turned into garden mulch. Even the milkies' and bakers' horses' droppings on the road outside were treasured.

'John, quick as you can, before the neighbours see it, grab the shovel by the back door. There's a beautiful big fresh pile right outside; put it straight in the kero tin and add some water. It makes the best liquid fertiliser. No point in asking Mary, you know what she's like.'

Despite Mary's shortcomings, I don't recall them ever having a cross word. Mary kept to herself. It was as though she wandered around the house in a world of her own, almost invisible. We kids all envied her ability to avoid work.

Amazingly Grandma's maid Mary drew no wages. Cleaning up Grandma's house years later, we found uncashed pension cheques and bank notes under the faded carpets. Typical of that generation, her pride was undiminished.

I don't know what happened to Mary in the end. As Grandma's memory faded so did Mary. Grandma got older and needed more and more help. Mary wasn't available, so she went into a nursing home where she slowly drifted away from us.

If Mary had actually existed, would things have been much different? Probably not.

I can still hear Grandma calling, 'Mary, Mary,' followed by, 'Oh darn, you know she's getting quite deaf lately. It's so hard to get good help these days. Slip up the street dear, and get your grandfather a paper, will you? You know where my purse is.'

How to Write a Book
(in 10 Weeks)

'Gran, you're never too old to do what you want to do,' I told her.

'Rubbish dear, what would you know? Anyway, I'm getting too old for much these days,' my grandmother blustered. 'Now when I was young, things were different.'

'How were they different?' I sighed, knowing the forthcoming answer perfectly well. I'd heard it often enough. Come to think of it, I knew most of her replies to nearly every imaginable question.

'The world went a lot slower and people had more time for a chat. These days, everything goes too fast. Fast cars, fast food, fast men. Where will it end, I wonder?'

Gran had a point there. My job as a kindergarten teacher kept me very busy and, what with having to keep my flat clean, clothing washed and the fridge stocked with food, there was little time or money left over.

'Well, you'll be pleased to know I'm thinking of doing a U3A course soon,' she continued.

'A what?'

'University of the Third Age, dear. I'm surprised you haven't heard of it, although U3A is somewhat geared to the elderly, I suppose. It'll be something for you to look forward to when you get older,' she said pointedly.

I had to admit that old age didn't appear that attractive. Everyone at Gran's old people's hostel seemed to be deaf, repetitive, forgetful or just plain old.

'So what's the course you're interested in, Gran?'

'I've decided to write a book!'

'A what?'

'You know dear, a book. You complain about my hearing, but I think you're the one with the hearing problem,' she chuckled. 'Maybe you should think about getting a hearing aid. That's what your mother is always going on at me about. When she deigns to visit me that is.'

'Touché, Gran.'

My grandmother smiled and continued, 'When your grandfather was alive, he always wanted to write a book about the two of us. That's why I need to do the course, to find out how to do it for him,' said Gran, leaning back in the chair quite pleased with herself.

'Welcome to the U3A course, "How to write a book in 10 weeks." I'm Alistair. I should point out that this course has a component which I take seriously and that I expect all of you to participate in fully, despite your age. Don't forget the saying, "Old age and treachery will beat youth and inexperience."

'In each week of the 10 week course I'll be setting homework in the form of parts of your book and I'll be expecting each of you to submit the homework for my perusal.'

A lot of the grey heads were now looking around at one another; the thought of homework still a daunting memory from when they were young.

'As a part of the course you are expected to be computer literate and internet access is preferred, as the homework has to be submitted to me weekly. For those who submit work personally, I will check your homework and hand it back the following week. For those who submit your submissions via the internet, I'll send any comments back via email within a day or so. Any questions so far?'

A sea of shocked and blank faces stared back at him.

'Now, the assessment of the course is, by its nature, continuous. Your completed book, or manuscript, as we fellow writers call it, will be the final assessment.'

When I next visited Gran, I hardly recognised her.

'I'll have to withdraw from the course, Alicia,' she sobbed. 'Seemed like a good idea at the time though. Always wanted to write a book, for your grandfather's sake, at least,' her watery eyes silently appealed to me. She said that the teacher seemed nice enough, at least for a high school setting. Apparently he was about my age and had only recently finished uni so he was in his first teaching post. Still, she hinted, he was easy on the eyes which I found to be an interesting comment from a 90 year old woman. Did she still look guys over after all these years?

Inwardly, I fumed. What sort of a teacher was he that

allowed vulnerable old folk to get into such a state? Even I knew that he should have checked out their computer literacy before letting them embark on such an ambitious undertaking. He'd got all their hopes up only to dash them. Now Gran was all upset. What a jerk he must be. Then I had an idea, but could I pull it off?

Tentatively I started, 'Gran, what would you think if I was to give you a bit of a hand with writing the book? You tell me what you want to say and I'll do the legwork. No one need know anything. What do you think?' My mischievous side surfaced, how I would love to play a neat prank on the condescending high school teacher.

So began the first assignment. My uni study came to the fore and soon we had the layout and preface written. Gran planned to record her courtship and marriage with my grandfather as the basis of her book, although sometimes I wondered if she wasn't giving me veiled hints about dealing with the opposite gender, something I'd had only limited success with. I noted that she had written down that old adage about 'Old age and treachery', something that the useless teacher had joked about, but much later I wondered if she hadn't outwitted me too.

Anyway, each week, she had to recall what the hopeless teacher wanted, dictate her story to me and all I had to do was enter the words, do a bit of editing, then submit the 'assignment' by email. Fortunately, I had a good laptop computer and a wireless modem to access the internet so we could make the most of my weekly visits to Gran's hostel. But I should have been better prepared for her teacher's comment after the first submission, 'Not bad for a beginner's work. Don't forget to try and engage the reader early in your book.'

I was furious and it took all my self control not to reply, telling him exactly what I thought of him. How dare he deride Gran's story. I found the story of Grandpa's courtship compelling and even racy at times. I hadn't realised that people in those days still faced the same quandary that we younger people do today, that of finding enduring love.

Each week now fell into a sort of pattern. On Gran's behalf, I had to submit a chapter or so of her book which she cheerfully dictated away to me. I decided to get the better of the teacher and began to make it into more of a love story with some social comment on the role of men. Keeping women barefoot and pregnant was hardly appropriate, I considered, even then.

Sure enough, into the net he came like a willing fish. Didn't she know 'men were only fulfilling expectations of society at the time?' he asked. What a Neanderthal he obviously was, I thought.

If that wasn't enough, the following week, he had the cheek to make the comment, 'Don't you think the female character is a little unbelievable?' I was, for once, speechless. Didn't he recognise that my Gran had braved the Great Depression followed by World War II, then raised a family on a worker's wage, losing her husband to a heart attack when he was only 50?

Who did this teacher think he was? Incensed, I returned to the computer and hammered out the next week's contribution. The poor old laptop keyboard really copped a bashing. Even Gran was amazed at my passion. In the story, I incorporated the notion that Gran, as the female character, had intelligence, stamina and courage, unlike some contemporary men, and strived to work alongside her husband as an equal, not just in a submissive role behind the scenes.

Well, that week, I seemed to have almost silenced the idiot critic at the other end of the email. His comment read, 'OK, point taken, now what about the male character?' With that concession I rubbed my hands in glee. My experience had been to find contemporary men dismally lacking in the ability to commit and were only looking for a good time. In truth however, my grandfather had been a little too fond of following the horses, so a large proportion of the family's meagre income had been squandered on the track. In her book, 'What was love?' I asked. 'Was it more than just a meeting of two hearts and minds?'

In due course, he countered with the intriguing comment, 'Maybe true love conquers all.' Hmm.

The following week, I mentioned modern women demanded more than Gran's generation received. On top of the list, I wrote respect, equality and appreciation, as pre-requisites for a modern woman such as Gran's granddaughter. Put that in your pipe and smoke it, I thought.

I wondered whether the teacher wasn't wising up to our ploy when he commented that the standard of Gran's work was exceeding all his expectations and 'showed maturity and wisdom coupled with relevance to present day values. By the way, the reference to your granddaughter makes captivating reading, a refreshing change to some of my pretentious and uncompromising female peers,' he also wrote. It seemed that this teacher wasn't going to be quite the pushover I had expected. Maybe I had met my match. Still, I liked a challenge.

The only concern I had now was Gran's health. Over the next few weeks I noticed that she was getting tired more easily and that her colour had paled; she could no longer attend the classes.

That week I entered Gran's thoughts on the computer but couldn't help wonder just how different our lives had been so far. She'd married at 16 and had her first baby by 18. That baby died and she went on to have seven more, although only four survived. It was so hard to reconcile the impact of contraception and improved health services these days. In my generation, women usually married around the age of 28 and had just over one child each in their early 30's with infant mortality terribly low in comparison. Many people now never even married or had any children. Then again, nowadays there appeared to be many single mums, existing on social security, with kids from more than one father. Divorce, almost unheard of in Gran's day, affected nearly half of my kindergarten's children, so they often grew up with only knowing one parent. So where did enduring love fit into the modern equation?

Now it seemed Gran herself was running out of steam. Over the last few days her skin colour had become pale, sometimes with a blue tinge to it. I guess that was why I was anxious to do whatever I could to fulfil what could be her last wish.

It was at the eighth week mark, with just two weeks before the end of the all important U3A course that I found her in bed when I called into the hostel on my weekly visit. She had a terrible colour. A thin plastic tube, attached to an oxygen cylinder alongside her, ran up to her nose. My loving grandmother and confidant was now in the final stages of heart failure.

Gran's eyes flickered open when I sat beside her bed and gently grasped her hand.

'How's the book going dear?' Her voice trembled, her breath sounding very wheezy.

'Fine, Gran, nearly done now. Only one more class to go,' I began with more hope than I felt. 'Don't know if I can finish it until you get better.'

'Alicia dear, I'm not sure I'll get better this time. It appears my heart's not what it used to be,' she wheezed. As Gran struggled to get her breath back, I saw she was trying to point to her bedside table drawer. Inside was an old battered diary, which I gathered that she wanted me to have.

'It's all in there,' she went on, 'I want you to finish the book for me.' A bit later her final words, weakly uttered to me were to, 'Make sure you thank Alistair for me in person, dear. It's very important.'

If ever there was a definition of 'odd man out', it had to be me at the U3A Graduation night. On the evening I was the youngest person there, surrounded by milling geriatrics in a sea of walking frames. But there was a distinct air of excitement in the room; this was obviously a highlight in their lives. How I wished Gran could have been there rather than me. I felt a real impostor.

I shuddered when I heard the request for the How to Write a Book class to assemble at the base of the stage. The announcer went on to mention that, 'as old Mrs Gardiner had recently passed away, her granddaughter will accept the certificate on her behalf.' As I walked very self consciously across the stage, I felt a pair of piercing brown eyes following me. His warm, firm hand gripped mine and shook it. I nodded my thanks and, head down, beat a hasty retreat.

After the presentation, Gran's teacher managed to leave the stage quickly and reached the exit just before me. He turned, barring my way and put his teacher's finger right under my chin. I felt him lift my head so no way could I avoid his steadfast and mesmerising gaze. It didn't help that my heart was pounding; I had to admit no guy had so easily affected me like this before. Maybe it was the occasion or that Gran had been right all along, I had to agree, he was kind of cute in an indefinable way.

'I know who you are, Alicia,' he started, 'and what you did,' he hinted, an ominous tone in his voice. 'I'm sorry about your grandmother, though.'

'Thanks,' I replied in a small voice. 'She wanted me to thank you for the course.'

He nodded his head, 'Your grandmother was a remarkable person, great strength of character ...' I went to continue walking around him on my way out but he kept talking, ' ... she was very proud of you and also asked me for a personal favour.'

'How does this concern me?' my curiosity was aroused.

'I was to take you out for a meal,' he explained, 'and I wasn't to be put off.'

With that, he scribbled a number on a piece of paper and passed it to me, 'When you're ready to take me up on the offer, just give me a call,' he hesitated before adding softly, 'please.'

I put off the inevitable for a week before I made the fateful call.

Open Wide

When Ginny the receptionist leaned around the corner into the surgery bearing her most exasperated look, Gene sensed a problem.

"Wing Seven at Villadale's got an emergency. Extreme facial pain, exposed nerve by the sound of it. Don't 'spose you can see her today?"

Villadale Detention Centre, that'd be bloody right. Wing Seven was the local high security women's section for illegal immigrants. And today of all days, a full schedule of crowns, cleans and fillings, not a spare spot. Gene sighed, even with a bit of juggling it would be yet another lost lunch time, and flying solo at that when his nurse took her lunch. As well Elena evidently had a boyfriend and often came back late with fresh love bites on her neck as though she'd just been attacked by an octopus.

At least the centre was ringing beforehand; many people walked in straight off the street and expected instant treatment. As if!

"OK, I'll squeeze her in. Tell them they have to have her here at midday on the knocker."

Typical government service contract, little notice, only paid the scheduled fee and tardy at that. Bloody refo queue jumpers all of them and still to learn the error of their ways. Gene wondered whether an impromptu lesson on Australian culture and ethics might be as necessary as repairing teeth. And wasn't he the one in an ideal position to deliver both? From a dental perspective, so to speak, not that many of them could.

Standing on one foot in the doorway, her hands nervously gripping one another, no way was the detainee exactly what he expected. Pommy over-stayer perhaps? Mostly they were dressed in drab detention garb, however this one wasn't. She must have come with the squeamish guard from last time who always refused point-blank to enter the surgery since she entered alone. Something to do with the shrill high-pitched drill, the guard had said at the time, grabbing the latest Cosmopolitan and disappearing into the adjoining waiting room.

"Name or number?" No point in pleasantries and Ginny could catch up on the paperwork afterwards.

"I'm Aleisha."

"Well, come on in, Aleisha, no time to waste." Gene reached out through the doorway, lightly guiding the patient's arm inside. At least this one was able to speak English.

"Jump in the chair now," he said.

He notices her hands cupping the left jaw, a dead giveaway.

Otherwise a brunette shock of hair partly disguising emerald eyes rested against a pert nose. A discrete waft of perfume, citrus maybe, nearly overcame the smell of his surgery's sterile disinfectant. Oh man, a 20-something patient, not much younger than his 25 years and seriously cute. Concentrate Gene, he told himself. Focus.

"Open wide."

Ah yes, there it was, tooth number 33, an incisor with a nasty broken cusp exposing the nerve pulp. Often very painful. Hmm, should he post, crown or extract? X-ray? No, maybe not needed.

To be frank, Gene had little sympathy for illegals, especially since his surgery had been broken into only three weeks before, the place left ransacked like a rubbish dump in the search for cash and drugs. Oh well, mustn't bear grudges, he thought, loading the syringe with Novocaine. But first a little local anaesthetic gel on the gum.

"Hold still now, nothing to worry about, you may just feel a little prick alongside your tongue." Was that a cough he felt from under him? With the blinding overhead light, her eyes were tightly screwed up in anticipation.

While the anaesthetic slowly infiltrated its numbing magic, he picked up cotton wads for alongside the gum, focussed the overhead light and noted the three minutes needed. Ah yes, nearly forgot the suction tube, but then his nimble fingers unusually fumbled the wads.

"Whoops." Could he quickly pluck them from her cleavage, his brow wrinkled, would she notice?

Aleisha suddenly squirmed.

"Sorry, thought there were two down there. Ah, there they are." Darn, that had never happened before, best he use a bib and keep going regardless. Great boobs though.

"Of course I have to wear rubber gloves; could be AIDS, hepatitis or STDs inside."

Puzzlement replaced her earlier grin.

"What are you in for?" he asked.

Initially hesitating, she garbled away, her face contorting as the word 'break' escaped unscathed. With cheeks puffed with cotton wads and a numb tongue that felt more like a doormat, most patients sounded unintelligible. An occupational hazard for dentists, English dialect by anaesthetic.

"Ah, breaking and entering." Of course, returning to the scene of the crime, he had heard it often happened. "Not very Ocker, Aleisha," he chastised. "Just relax, I'll be in and out before you know it. Let's make a start."

"We Aussies always respect each other's property. Souveniring, yes, theft, no," he added.

At this her eyes appeared to look a little disturbed, perplexed even.

As he began drilling, Aleisha's undivided attention was all his, maybe he could turn this wayward young lady around, into an ideal citizen. This detainee had a special air of innocence about her, as though she hadn't become disillusioned with Australia's immigration policies. Yet.

"Of course my last one had to be restrained in the chair with handcuffs."

Her eyes widened.

"Then she offered sex in the chair if I let her go out the back door, as if. Rinse and spit please."

Aleisha crossed her legs, glancing left and right in alarm, something he put down to the suction tube stuck on her tongue.

"Not before she accused me of looking down her blouse. Can you believe it?"

She squirmed uncomfortably, her hands flying up again under the bib.

Gene had drilled the posts, now for mixing the two part resin and the ultra-violet setting light.

"How long have you got to go?"

Aleisha's brows wrinkled.

"A well-deserved three months I would have thought,' he said, memories of the break-in flooding back. 'Of course in Singapore they use the birch. Something, along with others, I find quite appealing."

She rolled her eyes, and slowly shook her head. Right, so now he was getting through.

"You should aim to do something useful for this country. No, don't try to talk. You're young, attractive and you have great opportunities in front of you. Under different circumstances I'd even offer you a bed, Aleisha. You can rinse and spit again."

By now his patient was getting a little agitated, something he put down to the drilling close to the nerve and the need to work quickly. Anaesthetic didn't last forever.

"So what do you blame? Something you put in your mouth?"

After a pause she nodded.

"Drugs, of course. None here now. Anything else?"

The word 'broken' emerged along with a spray of saliva and remnants of drilled tooth. It wasn't easy juggling the suction pipe without a nurse. A river of dribble ran down her numb, slackened chin.

"Ah, broken home. Well, we could all use that excuse, couldn't we? My parents didn't even marry, so you can guess what I was called at school," he said, shaping the tooth surface.

Her head nodded vigorously in agreement.

"Oh boy, I'd kill for a coffee right now, you?"

When she nodded, he took this as affirmation she was indeed from criminal stock. Penal genes. Murder probably ran in her family's veins. What else did he expect from Villadale? How could she possibly be different?

"Not long now, soon you'll be back where you belong, in a cosy cell. Lightly close your jaw, very good, now open wide."

Gene peered in, "Of course you'll be thinking about payment. Well don't worry, it's free in Oz, all courtesy of you doing something naughty, possibly to the likes of me, eh?"

Her eyes took on a look close to desperation.

"Right," he said, straightening up, "now that wasn't so bad, was it? Remember not to eat on that tooth for 24 hours." His fingers gently prised open her talon-like grip on the chair's arm rests.

"Just got to pat you down, policy I'm afraid. Your ilk has been known to swipe my gear." Only last week Ginny's audit had shown several syringes and dental probes missing, probably used for illicit tattooing. Aleisha wriggled uncomfortably as his hands ran lightly over her body.

"And when you return for a follow-up I don't want to see you in those clothes. Come back when you're drug free and have got a visa."

With a lopsided mouth Aleisha mumbled incoherently, tears of relief bursting down her cheeks, and slipped out as quickly as she'd entered.

Ah yes, he was pleased, evidently his message had got through and the lost lunchtime would pay dividends for Australia.

Ginny stuck her head around the doorway.

"Your detainee patient is here now. Was held up in traffic, will I show her in?"

His mouth opened wide as if for inspection.

"What! Who was that then?" his eyes matched his cavernous mouth.

"Don't know, but you obviously made a big impression; she bolted out the door and left without paying!"

Maybe, Maybe Not

He looked different to how I'd last seen him at the brothel. A vivid scar now cratered his left cheek from chin to forehead. OK, he was also a little older, like me, with a couple of grey hairs amongst a brown curly mop. Was he wiser? Maybe, maybe not.

'Josh?'

An eye as brown as washed seaweed flicked over me, the other sightless eye stayed still.

'I know you, but I don't know you,' He replied.

'You were my 'buyer'.'

'Ah, that's right, my last one before they deported me. The pretty Aussie one, Alyssa, wasn't it?'

Soon described as a 'white slave' in Amsterdam, all I fuzzily remembered was a free drinks evening in a sleazy nightclub and the faint prick of a needle in my arm. My next recollection was of bright lights in a bare, barred room and an excruciatingly slow realisation that my life was never going to be the same again. And it wasn't. Oh no, it definitely wasn't.

After I was broken in, an indescribable journey to hell and back, my 'trainer' taught me that abject compliance to all men meant a meal ticket for me, some money and my passport. One day, maybe.

Freedom vanished.

Brutal smelly men, unremitting, painful to the extreme ... and I complied, eventually. My depravity knew no depth. Then I lived for the daily needle (little else eased the internal pain), all the time cursing my desire to experience the world alone by backpack. What had I been thinking? It had been a lifelong dream of seeing places, meeting people. Not the nightmare it became. My folks thought me dead, while I wondered when would they finally give up hope?

Freedom, ah yes, what was that again?

I thought I'd never see it again, until the day a blurry tanned face with a familiar flat accent from home appeared in front of me. 'I want her, the pretty one,' a voice said. Like I'd been trained, I thrust my bony hips out, pouted my lips and angled my youthful pointed breasts towards him, hoping he wouldn't see my needle-tracked arm. What was a fellow Aussie doing in a place like this, buying a girl like me? A druggy white slut, weren't the punters all the same?

But something about this one was strange. He led me away to a faraway room, and inside, reached up to unscrew the globe. When the buyer thrust my passport and a thick handful of paper Euros into my hand, flicking his finger dismissively, I hesitated only a few seconds before taking them. What did I have to lose?

'Go home,' he said.

And so I did.

But now I was back home, seven years older, clean and oh so much wiser. Not content, just wiser. Finding Josh had become my goal. I had a nice flat, work, money in the bank but still I kept checking, searching, following leads, looking. Had it been a curse to be considered pretty? For me, maybe, maybe not. Where was he? Where was my liberator? All I had was a first name and a face, but what had he really wanted with me? Little did he know finding him had transgressed from frustrated curiosity to an obsessive search. In some cultures, saving a life meant a lifetime of moral debt. I was now clean and healthy, but why was I here? I needed to find Josh. What had he really wanted? Why me?

'So?' I asked.

'You still had some spirit, a bit like my sister,' he said with a wry smile, adding, 'I see you made it back OK.'

'I want to know who you are. Tell me about yourself.'

And he did.

'You were the last one we freed before they found us,' he said. 'I always wondered how you'd got on.'

'How did you make it happen?'

'A friend did the inside work, passports and so on. I played the part of a customer. We did OK until they caught up with us. Got eight away, including you,' he paused. 'But my mate Ralph didn't get out.'

I gulped. 'Why did you do it?'

'No one should be held captive,' his voice petered out, choking, 'especially not women.'

'I owe you my life,' as my hand found his, 'Thanks.' A determined but compassionate hand, why was I not surprised?

I wondered, would he see more than his sister in me? Maybe, maybe not, we'd see.

Collaborative Consumption

'Using stuff we already have to get the stuff we want – all without accumulating more stuff.'

Losing your job may be considered nearly the ultimate in carelessness but being made redundant attributes no blame, does it?

Upon reflection, the payout letter appeared generous, the formula giving the longest term employee an entitlement close to a year's salary. Too bad I had left my previous job not long before on the promise of better pay. Now I was unemployed, broke and despairing.

Tramping from one job interview to another I had plenty of time to wonder whether the GFC had taken another victim – trust! Times are tough, they said. Uncertainty rules, they said. Come back in a few months, they said, Normally we'd snap you up, they said. The words wore down my self confidence like a block of cheese against a grater. I felt crumbly.

It was the article in the magazine that provided my second ray of hope. I say second, because the first stole my CD collection, camera, phone and laptop computer, escaping after a month without paying a single cent of board. 18 year old bitch! On the bright side, most of my stories were indelibly etched word for word in my 28 year old grey matter. Maybe they needed re-editing anyway.

Trust, what was that again?

This time I decided not to use a handwritten note in the corner shop window, but an authenticated Internet website dedicated to collaborative dealing, guaranteed and fully insured. For those not yet into the latest electronic fad, the website had a checklist of items in demand along with a rough price guide. For instance, my spare car space, once it was cleared out of kerbside junk that is, would be worth about $20 a week for someone looking to park their car off the busy street.

But did I really want to share all my earthly possessions, let alone my life, with just any old stranger?

Meantime the pressure of being a month behind on my mortgage mounted. How rude was the bank's demand, saying that the periodic payment had failed 'due to insufficient funds' and another default would initiate more urgent action. 'Tell me something I don't know,' I yelled out loud.

In the end, I listed two rooms of my house for rent at $150 per week, my old but trusty Mazda MX5 at $200 per week, the car space at $20 per week and a weekly meal for $20. Then, to keep food on the table a garage sale netted $230 and mowing lawns in the street another $120. Suddenly I was rich, sort of. Next step, the deal I made with myself was that if I was still jobless after a month, I'd put my place, a 'renovator's delight' and the house of my dreams, on the market.

Last step, renting, yet again.

Ping. 'New mail', the message flashed onto my screen. At least the contents insurance claim had come through, especially when I had pleaded the 'tools of the trade' clause, my laptop computer.

OK, what did I have? I squinted at the computer screen. A 20 year old male music student wanting room and full board. Did I want 8 hours of trombone practice daily? I don't think so. A 46 year old tattoo artist but with the last 12 months of his life unaccounted for - hmm, jail? I wondered, clicking onto the next and last applicant. Wow, Kieran Forsyth, a 30 year old university sociology lecturer on exchange wanted the lot for six months and would I do a bulk deal for $500 per week or exchange for similar in London?

My fingers trembled as they clicked on 'reply'.

'Need cash not exchange. Please send references and photos,' I typed.

'No can do. Photo, webcam camera on the blink. Month's rent in advance in lieu OK? Send bank details,' she replied at the speed of light.

I hesitated for 14 megapixels, nanoseconds, minibytes or whatever and agreed before she changed her mind.

With the money electronically transferred, suddenly a trip to the bank seemed like a visit to the beach: my decline into penury, bankruptcy and possible new career as a hooker had been staved off with only days to spare. My collaborator was to arrive in a couple of days, could I do a pick up at the airport?

Better still, my career descent was seemingly arrested. At one company I got shortlisted and another rang my references. Could my job fortunes have begun to arrest in a U turn?

Why had I agreed to an airport collection, I asked myself over and over.

'Shit,' he said, 'you're a woman! Sam?'

'The last time I looked, and holy shit, Keiran,' I responded in kind, 'you're a guy.' We must have looked at one another for fully a minute, me giving in first. How had this debacle come about? What was I to do? No way could his money be returned nor could he find another place at such short notice. It seemed we were stuck with one another and would have to make the most of it. After all, his references were impeccable. Maybe having a male in my house would work out; it was only for six months after all. What could possibly go wrong?

We'd only just got home when it started. Six months, I despaired.

'Of course I'll need the bathroom in the mornings,' he said, as with a marble in his accent.

'In your dreams, you pommy pretender,' I exploded. 'This is no longer a penal colony. It's my bathroom and I use it in the mornings. You can have it at night.'

His open mouth said it all. He was obviously used to having it all his way, but no longer. Turning my back I walked away.

A week into our 'collaboration' and things were still not going well. The existence of people like Kieran seemed to me to be a good reason to be glad the UK was in the northern hemisphere and furthermost from Australia. Republic? It couldn't come fast enough.

'I say, Sam,' he started, 'this sauce would be better with a little more salt.'

'Here, Kieran,' I said, putting a dollop on my spoon,' 'add it yourself.' The dollop flew across the table and landed right on his forehead before falling onto his plate. A brilliant shot, exceeding all my expectations.

'I say,' he exclaimed.

'Sorry,' I replied, 'my hand must have slipped.'

But then again that night as I pored over my résumé, he leant over and began to type and click.

'You can't,' I began. 'Oh, I see, right.' And much later, 'Hmm.'

Alright so the guy was a wordsmith, or was it his mouth breathing close to my ear? And why wouldn't he steal a kiss, oh right he just did. On the forehead? Just what did I expect?

Nevertheless at the end of five months I was ready to strangle my collaborator, a more frustrating man I hadn't met. Pompous, self opinionated about everything except his emotions but an absolute whiz in the kitchen, he'd sabotaged my efforts for employment, saying he needed someone to do his secretarial stuff, was I for hire? Kitchen, office or bedroom I was tempted to ask. Office it was. Right.

Then, all those months later, came a call that was to change our collaboration. His father was dying, could he return home ASAP? With his project nearly at a close, one minute he was there, next minute gone. All that remained was a forgotten shaver, the final month's rent with the bond thrown in as a bonus. Wow! What was I meant to do with unexpected windfall? Despite this I was devastated, who was there to listen to me whinge now? I kinda missed him, loathe as I was to admit it.

'Hi Kieran.' In the midst of the crowded Heathrow terminal his greying head stuck out. Or so it seemed.

'Sam. What kept you? Now, as I was saying, the secret to a perfect soufflé is to use cold eggs.'

My jaw dropped. Was I that predictable? Here I was 10 thousand kilometres from home and wondering why.

'So how's your father?' I said after kissing him hello. After a moment he kissed me back, with a passion that needed some work on. Still, I liked a challenge.

'Passed away, I'm afraid,' he said. 'Very regrettable, yes, very sad.'

'I'm so sorry,' my arms wrapped around him. Just why was I doing that? Did jetlag from Australia make one delusional? Or remove inhibitions?

'Yes, well,' he said, somewhat embarrassed, grabbing my bag. 'Now I seem to have mislaid my shaver. Have you seen it?'

'In my bag. But Kieran, where am I staying, with you?'

Was he accountable? 'Of course, don't you trust your collaborator?' he winked.

No, I didn't. And if he wasn't visiting my bed and dreams that night, I was visiting his. No longer would mutual procrastination keep us apart.

The Legend of
Bulldust Bill

Starting an apprenticeship at an impressionable 16 not only did I learn a lot about motor mechanics but also much about life. In those heady days of Australia in the 1980's, if you had brains you went to Matriculation and probably university. If you wanted to work with your hands, it required starting a trade after Form Four, if you were fortunate enough to get an apprenticeship.

Being an apprentice meant that in the first year you swept floors and made the coffee, and in the second year you washed parts. Third year was spent passing the tools while the fourth year meant you actually wielded spanners in anger. Bulldust? Well, maybe just a sprinkling - a foot deep.

Apart from the usual pranks of being sent for a long weight, collecting a tin of sparks from under the grinder and looking for a left-handed hammer, the legend of Bulldust Bill was bandied about in many a work conversation. 'Bill could do that with his eyes closed,' they'd say to me, as I tried to remove the furthest spark plug that was buried somewhere beyond reach. 'Of course, Bill could undo that with his little finger,' was what others would comment while I was sweating at the end of a six foot bar on a seized axle nut. 'A boy could serve a four year apprenticeship in a week working under Bill,' they'd say. Oh how I wished that this was possible; maybe then I could afford to pay off my tools. Apprentice wages were way less than university study allowances but after the indenture you could earn about a quarter of a doctor's wage or an eighth of a dentist's, with a little luck.

Over the next few years, as I gained experience around the suburban workshops of Melbourne, it appeared that the renowned Bill had also worked in many places, his legendary mechanical prowess preceding him like a shock wave. Fast? Some even suggested he had six fingers on each hand and could do up nuts so quickly they'd weld themselves tight with the friction. Clever? One guy even said Bill could tune twin carburettors with bare toes and tighten the fan belt at the same time. Right! And strong, at fully seven, no, eight feet tall he never used jacks, just bodily lifted the corner of the car up and kicked the stands underneath with his foot. Smart? All he had to do was have the phone put next to the exhaust and, hey presto, an instant diagnosis. As for the latest in electronics, they said Bill could put his giant hands across the battery and sense what was going on in the engine's computer by the tingle in his fingers. Farfetched? How were we to know otherwise? Would Aussie mechanics feel the need to embellish the story of a real-life legend?

As life would have it, our head mechanic had a heart attack, the workshop was short-handed, so the legendary Bill was to start first thing Monday morning. The three of us couldn't believe our good fortune. No job application or references needed for Bill, his reputation was beyond question. Yes, we were to have the legend himself working alongside us! That Friday there was a buzz of excitement throughout the workshop. The floors were scrubbed through two layers of grime back down to the concrete and rusty benches were wiped until they shone. Even the outside dunny got the royal treatment – with a new deodoriser tablet in the cracked bowl and last year's phonebook for paper, it was obvious the boss was sparing no expense. Even the lunchroom table was cleared of dog-eared girlie magazines and the car seats we used had some old curtains thrown over to hide the sharp exposed springs.

'Get a haircut and make sure you wash your overalls over the weekend,' the boss yelled to us as we left. 'William's going to put this workshop on the map for once.' William? And we thought Bulldust Bill was coming!

Certainly Bill was tall; he carried a tool box under each arm and strode confidently up to the boss, his piercing blue eyes missing little. With his dinner plate sized hands he insisted on shaking everyone else's. All the guys grimacing in turn, except myself when I feigned having hand-wash on them. Finally, we would get to see the legend in action, someone I had aspired to emulate all my 24 years.

Then it started.

What hadn't travelled with the legend was Bill's extensive use of unimaginable expletives; he was like a one man football team at grand final time. Without warning he would let loose at the top of his voice the foulest language including every rude word known to mankind. No one was immune from the verbal abuse. No person and no occasion was sacred. Once a customer strayed into the workshop to get something from his car but hastily beat a retreat when Bill angrily suggested he 'combine sex and travel and f … off.' We were flabbergasted at this development. Why hadn't this strange characteristic accompanied his reputation?

The boss only let Bill loose with the phone once.

Unfortunately it was the local minister's wife Bill had abused, by telling her she was 'Satan's slut and should be burnt at the bloody stake.' It took a sizeable donation into the church restoration fund to smooth that transgression over, believe me.

After that the boss kept Bill on a tight leash, right away from hearing distance of the phone and anyone else. Lack of contact with the customers, spare parts guys and salespeople left Bill isolated, something he appeared not to mind. He still swore profusely, like a politician, at the least provocation and sometimes without, but I wondered if maybe he could concentrate more on the actual job without being distracted. His work output was prodigious; unlike us, he never grumbled at his lean wage packet or that the boss drove a Lamborghini while we qualified for low income tax assistance. Elspeth, the boss' wife, spent a third of her life at the local hairdresser, another third with a personal trainer doing whatever trainers do, and the last third at a cosmetic surgeon.

So we had to work hard.

Rumour had it that Bill had been married 20 years before but his wife had died giving birth in a taxi that had broken down on its way to the hospital. Maybe this explained his quest for perfection in repairs. Apparently he had raised their daughter by himself, guarding her like his tools, not trusting a single soul. I only saw the daughter once, driving Bill home after work. I gave her a friendly wave. She had an attractive face and she hesitated, then smiled before waving back. Hmm.

There wasn't a bolt or nut Bill couldn't undo, or an engine

or gearbox too heavy, and yet he had a woman's gentlest touch when needed, no thread did he ever strip. An intuitive mechanic in diagnostics left him without peer. It was as though he thought mechanically; every move seemed planned and systematic. Certainly I never saw him make a mistake. Sheer genius. Watching and learning, I was in total awe.

Except for the language.

Bill had been with us for about a month when one day the boss' wife dropped off his lunch, 'tidying up' the strategically-placed parts on a bench on her way past. Oh dear; we waited with bated breath for his reaction and we weren't disappointed. After Bill had yelled out to all and sundry that the boss' wife was 'an interfering bitch' and 'a lying whore who belonged in a brothel', the boss' patience was under pressure.

'You'll have to sack him, Herbert,' Elspeth said, her face Botox-frozen in anger.

For the boss it was the last straw, he was facing a very cold bed at night otherwise.

'Bill, I have to let you go,' he said, gulping, as the giant towered a full foot overhead and moving closer with clenched fists, "but because I'm a fair man, how about a week, no, a month's wages in lieu of notice?' From a boss tight as a fish's bum, this was unheard of generosity.

That night we all lined up to say farewell and survive another bone crushing handshake. As the youngest I was the last in line. Wearing a thick leather welding glove I faced my hero; could I ever hope to emulate his mechanical prowess?

'All the best, Bill,' I said, quietly adding after everyone was out of earshot, 'but I think you've got Tourette's syndrome.'

'What?' he shouted as I braced for an outburst.

'It's a disease of the central nervous system; involuntary vocalisations. Maybe you should see a doctor.'

'Thanks mate,' he whispered, clapping me on the shoulder, 'Listen, want to come home for tea? We always have fish and chips Friday night Marie and I don't get many visitors.' Then giving me another once over, 'You must have read the same book, but how else would I get to work only half the year and be paid what I'm worth?'

Dog, a Man's Worst Fiend

BANG! Then a second later, BANG! Following the explosions came a series of muffled curses from under the house and then suddenly a brown mass, closely resembling a mobile door mat, rocketed out from under the house. The mongrel dog had turned into a brown blur. As the acrid smell of gunpowder wafted up the gaps in the lino-covered floorboards, a tell-trail of blood dotted the cracked concrete footpath leading up the street and out of sight.

With a shrug of pride Dad gently rested the shotgun against the back door, dusted himself off and, spring in his step, headed in for afternoon tea. Well briefed, we kids, hanging around in the faint hope of receiving melting butter on a crusty hot scone, pretended nothing had happened as a few neighbours drifted out to their front gates to see what was going on, curious looks on their faces. Always friendly to everyone, we waved reassuringly and hoped no one complained. Soon a lost tranquillity returned to our suburban weatherboard fibro home, and if the paint peeled a little who cared?

Living behind a butcher's shop in Devon Street proved to be a mixed blessing. Sure, we could always run there at the last moment before tea for a forgotten chop or sausage but the butcher's customers had also been known to block our driveway. Either way, our usual diet of tongue, kidneys, liver, tripe, and brains was always conveniently served from the butcher's shop. Offal? More like awful. We hardly needed a refrigerator, buying daily for perishables with a grocer only a few yards further away proving to be another advantage of living next to Croydon's main street.

It appeared the butcher's shop attracted two species, Homo sapiens and Canis lupus familiaris; but it was the latter that caused us the most problems. Man's best friend? No way, more like our worst nightmare.

Dad claimed a good pet had to be useful. That's why we had chooks, for eggs, so the unproductive hen was destined to become our next meal. When I queried his budgies' value, he sidestepped the issue with the fact that they were mainly fed on spoil from the vegie patch. After that I dared not question the family cat's errant life, especially as he spent most nights purring on Dad's knee. Like my two sisters, who did as they were told, I sat up, ate up and shut up. Life was simple. Do as you were told and nothing went wrong.

Dogs were specifically excluded from our family for two reasons besides being unproductive, they cost money to feed and would have hampered our school holiday plans.

'Roy? Did you hear all that noise last night?' was my mother's greeting the following morning.

My father didn't answer, his mouth full of a split second breakfast. He was 15 minutes away from school time and facing a 15 minute drive to get there. The car usually started easily, except when it didn't and then he was late. Dad was not a morning person.

'Sounded like dogs under the house,' Mum continued unfazed, 'made a terrible racket. I'm amazed the whole neighbourhood didn't hear them.'

Typical of the post-war era, Mum was a stay-at-home mum. Indeed, earlier on she was lucky enough to have kept her bank job after marriage due to all the men who had enlisted. When the surviving men returned in '45 and she fell pregnant with my elder sister, her job disappeared entirely though.

'Later, dear, got to get to work,' Dad yelled halfway out the door, still eating his toast. With luck his Grade Six class would be at assembly, a few minutes absence unnoticed.

After a few more sleep interrupted nights I was instructed to accompany Dad on an inspection around the house. Sure enough, piles of raw aromatic dirt and paw prints abounded, the evidence of a dog or dogs, despite there being barge boards all around the house. Several hours later, much sawing and hammering, punctuated by much bad 'not inside the house, son' language, saw the house rendered almost bulletproof. Even the fences were reinforced, but the driveway proved tricky, the gates having been removed for speedy departures. 'Slows a man right down getting to work', Dad had said. I nodded agreement. This was the 50's where a teenage son thought his father a hero until proved otherwise. Rarely did a situation or person get the better of him, unlike his 13 year old son, me.

When the dogs returned in earnest the following week, the family began to take a more personal interest. Lost sleep was difficult to make up, arguments became more frequent, wild accusations flew thick and fast and even a few fights developed. Everyone was suffering sleep deprivation while seemingly a pack of wild dogs was woofing, barking and yelping under our beds. I wondered whether they were doing what dogs did on the Croydon High School oval. Our art classroom overlooked the oval affording everyone a great view, but our teacher had declined the opportunity for a free biology lesson on dogs' reproductive habits and hastily pulled the curtains.

'Back to painting everyone,' she'd yelled with a red face, muttering under her breath, 'no morals.' I think she was referring to the dogs.

Tired, my mother was not exempt from bad temper, unable to resist goading Dad into further action.

'Can't you do anything about those dogs, Roy?' she demanded. 'Shouldn't be so difficult I would have thought.'

Dad fumed.

Mum continued as only she could, 'Surely you could hammer on a few more boards?'

Little did she know Dad had used up every skerrick of spare wood, the sides of the house resembling a boat rather than a house. Still the wretched dogs dug in inspirational form, nothing was going to stop them from their night concerts under our house. High pitched whining, with an occasional 'woof' just as you were falling asleep were part of their night-time chorus a few inches under the wooden floorboards. Scampering and scratching their way around our stumps, the dogs slowly drove us insane.

The next step taken in the dog's debacle occurred when Dad decided to enlist the authorities' assistance. This decision was not one he took lightly as he had a poor view of the local council, his diatribes about their activities or lack thereof occupying many a meal time conversation.

'I'll look into it and see what I can do, Mr Pitman,' Bryant, the local by-law officer said. 'Not easy to catch stray dogs you know.'

Dad agreed, but privately suggested that Bryant's expansive girth was the real reason for his lack of success.

A week and several phone calls later Bryant admitted the dog problem was proving more difficult than he had envisaged. The council had issued him with a six foot long pole with a noose on the end. Something more suited to the middle ages, the pole barely extended past his waist. Combined with the dog's speed, he struggled to catch his own breath.

'It's the butcher's shop, Roy,' he conceded, now on first name terms. 'I think the dogs are getting the bones from behind the shop and having a feast under your house. Of course it could be a bitch on heat.'

I gasped at his language until I remembered he was probably referring to a female dog.

'Any chance of getting the Health Inspector onto it?' asked Dad, barely keeping his patience in check with local council protocol. This situation wasn't helped by Bryant usually letting the butcher's customers who parked across our driveway off with the slap of a wet lettuce leaf, or so Dad said.

'Could be tricky, different department, you see, but I'll look into it,' was his reply, prompting Dad to rename him Mr Mirror at the tea table that night. Bryant was living up to his reputation when once he looked into something nothing eventuated.

'Action, not looks, is needed,' Dad ranted.

We kids agreed, anything for a good night's rest.

After another sleep interrupted week, Mum and Dad were hardly talking, marital relations were being strained. Why couldn't Dad do something, Mum nagged, instead of just talking about the bloody dogs all the time. What was the good of men if they couldn't do something? Dad seethed, but not silently. We kids made ourselves scarce, extra household chores being loaded onto anyone within reach. Mum rarely swore but the nightly cacophony of baying dogs was now of neighbourhood volume. Normally a deathly quiet residential area, the barking and howling made our house sound like a kennel.

Always one for lateral thinking, Dad decided to take matters into his own hands. These errant dogs demanded action. For once Mum gave conditional approval provided he was careful and no one got hurt. Mum loved all of us in her own unique way and we assumed she included Dad in that group, although there were times ...

The borrowed 12 gauge shotgun was awe inspiring, its long grey metal barrels and polished wooden butt grabbed my fertile imagination sharpened by the fearless Biggles, wartime pilot extraordinaire. I was even allowed to hold the unloaded gun, that was amazingly heavy, briefly. Wow! What havoc Captain Bigglesworth and his companions Ginger and Algy could have caused with this war relic.

'Are you sure it's safe?' my mother, always the Doubting Thomas, started, 'looks very dangerous.'

An exasperated husband replied, 'I thought you wanted the dog problem to go away? For Christ's Sake woman, what do you expect me to do?'

'So what did Bryant say?' Mum asked, not fazed by Dad's comment.

'Considering I'm doing his damn job for him, not much. Provided there're no complaints, Bryant said he'd turn a blind eye.'

This was an expression I understood well, along with, 'You're only in trouble if you get caught.' It seemed the family was finally on a winner. Dad would shoot the dog, we'd all get a full night's sleep and I'd have a good tale to tell my school mates for once. Inwardly I cheered my brave father; no shirker was he of tackling a tough job.

That day brand-new Eveready batteries were put in the torch. This was another indication that he meant business. Dad donned his old dark blue overalls, their RAAF insignia nearly all worn away.

'Threw them out at the end of the war, son,' Dad had told me confidentially, 'not needed anymore.'

A teacher at enlistment, he had been trained as an aircraft wireless mechanic during the war. Our workshop was full of similarly 'unwanted' items from when he, along with most others, was demobilised in '45 and resumed teaching.

'Anyway,' Dad continued, 'a bit of souveniring is not like stealing, if you get my drift.'

I did. Along with a couple of other kids we'd been 'souveniring' soft drink bottles from the back of Gibson's café until Mr Gibson fixed the broken palings. Amazing what lollies those souvenirs bought when we redeemed their own bottles across the front counter. Beat a non-existent pocket money any day.

Now it seemed as though our father was entering a dangerous wartime mission again. As it was a weekend afternoon, we were all hanging around like blowflies, even a little excitedly. Dad loaded the double barrelled shotgun in front of us, the red and brass cartridges glinting.

'Do you really need two shots?' Mum queried.

'Probably not Bubs, but better to be safe than sorry, eh? Kills at 20 yards, how can I miss? Be all over in seconds. The dog won't know what hit it.' They were indeed prophetic words.

In awe, we three kids all stood around as Dad stealthily headed out down the side of the house and around the back. Like a ferret down a rabbit burrow, our fearless father slid under the low house. With him rode all our hopes for a dog-less house and our father's safe return. Underneath the house, nothing could be heard except the occasional whine of a dog, something we were confident would soon become only a distant memory.

After the shooting, life seemed dull, even boring. Each night our sleep was complete, now I had no excuse not to do my homework, something that inspired me little. On the other hand, a go at that shotgun would have made my life complete.

Our parents started smiling at one another again and Dad even got to school on time several times running. He was now universally our family hero, who had bravely taken on the enemy and won resoundingly. Weren't our peaceful evenings proof? Life was good and we all started to look forward to camping on the next school holidays with anticipation. It was the Pitmans, one, two, three, as we lined up in front of our proud parents in our pyjamas at bedtime.

The butcher's shop reverted to attracting people not dogs and life went on as before, almost.

It must have been 10 or 12 days later that the first family member passing through our back door noticed something strange. But because it initially came and went without reason, no one worked out what it was. The smell could be put down to any number of our pets. After all we had budgies, 'Maybe the aviary needs cleaning out, Roy,' and chooks, 'Maybe the run needs cleaning out, Roy,' and a cat, 'Has someone got a present from Toddles on their shoe?'

Incrementally the faint waft became a persistent smell, the smell became a hideous stench, soon the situation became undeniably bad.

'I think something's died, Roy,' my mother exclaimed with authority the next meal time, possessing a rare talent to state the obvious. 'There's a terrible smell at the back door.' Mum had grown up on a farm and knew all there was to know about animal smells, so she told us.

Our permanently locked front door was never used, the back door being more convenient to the kitchen, the nerve centre of the house. Whenever visitors came, it was to the kitchen they gathered, thinking nothing of standing there whilst meals were prepared, dispensed and cleaned up. A smell at the back door had distinct ramifications, everyone would cop it, no one could avoid it.

Our family, especially at mealtimes, was an open family, otherwise known as 'brutally honest', where everything was discussed, substitute 'argued', at great length: politics, religion, school, no subject was spared. All of us hypothesized what might have gone wrong under the house. No one disputed that the dogs had something to do with the stench; no one was stupid, no one was wrong.

Dad looked every part the beaten man when he climbed once more into the old overalls. Maybe it was my mother's 'Can't you do anything right?' that contributed to his demeanour. Overnight he'd aged ten years. A handkerchief around his face, he slithered under the house, his nose and now flickering torch his only aids in locating the smell. I crouched alongside the gate ready to act or relay orders.

'Get a briquette bag, son,' came the terse words we feared most. It confirmed our worst fears that the dog had returned to our house to die under our back doorstep, the foul smelling, rotting carcass the final insult of its fiendish existence. 'And a spade, the long handled one.'

It got worse.

Dad muttered and cursed under the sharp splintered joists and bearers, his head caked in cobwebs and bruises. The dog had fought until the end and then some. Suddenly an expletive combining sex and purgatory rent the air. The dog's tail had come off in his hand! Now the spade was necessary to 'manoeuvre' the corpse, seething and mobile with maggots, onto the bag for disposal. Outside, I relayed the gruesome news, the family initially sympathetic with the unfolding pathos before hysterically laughing at the thought of the dog's defiant tail held upright in Dad's hand.

We buried the dog remains in the backyard. The hole's depth was hampered by Dad's one-handed grip on the shovel as he used the other one to pinch his nose closed against the corpse's smell. With the stomach wrenching stench neither was very far from nausea but eventually Dad rested on the spade. From his upright stance he proclaimed victory over the canine foe so we went inside for tea where an almost mute family sat.

'Well, that's that then,' my mother proclaimed, a note of triumph in her voice, now an expert on dogs and their peculiar habits. 'Of course, if ...'

To this day, I can remember the look that transpired between my parents at that moment. It signified a demarcation point, a type of marital cease-fire, an acceptance that the world was far from perfect and maybe one should let dead dogs lie. That night's meal was eaten in relatively silent contemplation.

The saga didn't end there, although it wasn't for the want of wishing it had.

A few nights later, the rest of the nuisance dogs returned, the shallow carcass too good an attraction to refuse.

Dad woke up at the sound of distant barking outside and realised what had happened. This was the first time I realised that my father was mortal, a man who sometimes made mistakes, someone I would follow in making mistakes. It's called growing up and lasts a lifetime.

Dad and I took turns in digging the new hole. When the hole got halfway up the spade handle and when I nearly fell in the grave, we dug no more. The remains of the dog, now heavily gnawed and mangled, were shovelled into the cavernous hole whereupon Dad poured a whole can of mower fuel on top, no expense spared. With an enormous 'Whomp!' the funeral pyre erupted into flame and burnt seemingly for ages. In respect to the animal's spirit, and due to a terrible pungent odour, we stood upwind. Then, as the flames diminished to a smoky flicker, we silently filled the pit in. No words were necessary; I had begun to enter the world of men. Mum would have crucified him if she knew what had happened.

So a word of advice, from experience you could say: choose your home site carefully, and unless you like dogs, don't live next door to a butcher.

Caught Out, Court In

Someone even the police didn't have a photo of, an elusive cat burglar, was proving a festering boil on the media image of the Police Commissioner; however my part in crime solving could be attributed to a brief lapse in memory.

'Sorry, mate, but can you turn back?' I said to the turbaned taxi driver, 'I've forgotten my digital voice recorder.'

His dark face turned to me. Alright, he hadn't understood a word so I mimicked a U turn with my fingers. Nearly an hour late for the conference dinner and keynote speech but I'd probably heard it all before anyway.

'Velly bad place for clime,' he said, spinning us around.

Staying at my mother's had seemed like a good idea at the time. Now classed inner suburban, her old two storey Edwardian house was located a few suburbs from the city conference venue so we could see each other in the evenings.

It must have been the faintest glimmer of light flashing through the stained glass panelling beside the front door that alerted me. A torch-wielding thief came to mind immediately. My old key slid into the well-worn lock noiselessly and I crept inside, wondering if my imagination had been hijacked by fatigue. Jet lag could do that to a person. Strange, I could have sworn I'd left the hall light on too. With back flattened against the hallway wall, I let my eyes adjust to the dark. No, I was right, as a darkened shadow flittered across my path, I saw a pencil torch being held out. Instincts from adolescent footy training kicked in and I launched a perfect spear tackle that would have made my old coach proud.

As the burglar went down like a bag of sand, my surprise attack was complete and I heard breath explode out from underneath me as his body took our combined weight on the moth-eaten hall carpet. With my knee firmly held in the small of his back, I continued the initiative of a textbook capture and began to frisk the thief for weapons. Many a householder has been hurt, killed even, by a crazed, armed burglar and I didn't want my mother or myself to be the next victim. His legs and pockets were clear but it was the chest area that gave me the first cause for concern. Either the thief had a bad case of 'man boobs' or 'he' was a 'she.' My fingers deftly encountered soft, smallish, but still shapely, breasts. First the right, then the left, then the right again, just to be sure, alright? Oh gosh, was that a nipple too? It didn't help that the body underneath mine was squirming vigorously either. I fantasised for a second, but only a second, I swear. Then logic took over, a female cat burglar, surely not? But yes, they were definitely breasts, a little flattened by my weight but it appeared I had caught me a lithe, female crim.

A muffled voice floated up from the carpet. Ever so carefully I released some of my knee pressure, just enough to hear her words.

'When you've finished groping,' she wheezed, 'or if you're going to rape me, hurry up and get it over with please. I'm busting to go to the loo.'

I couldn't help grinning. 'Rape, never. Caught out, yes. I'm the victim here.'

A grunt came from underneath me and her breathing was still wheezy. Apart from the heavily dust-laden carpet, there was another reason we couldn't stay like this much longer, my old footy knees were killing me. Still, I made a mental note to organise a house cleaner in to reduce the level of dust.

'Listen up, if I get off you, do I have your word you're not going to run away?'

Letting my words sink in, I took her silence as agreement.

'I want to talk to you. Then we'll discuss what course of action to take, OK?'

Another grunt.

Opportunistic to the extreme, I reasoned she must have waited until I'd left to break in taking advantage of my mother's refusal to wear a hearing aid. Quite audacious really, considering the house was occupied, albeit by an old lady who would have heard nothing. But then that was often the burglar's modus operandi, if I recalled correctly. One old couple had even been having afternoon tea on their patio when the burglar had robbed their bedroom just a few metres away. Their family jewellery disappeared forever, quite heartbreaking really, to traumatise defenceless oldies.

Disgruntled, the taxi driver took off leaving a cloud of evil smelling exhaust behind, but not before he snatched my proffered money. Wondering if the burglar had broken her word and slipped out the back, I returned inside.

I switched on the kitchen light but nothing happened. Darn! Then it dawned on me. Of course, the burglar, who was now dusting herself off, must have tripped the outside meter box killing all the lights, not that my mother, living alone, had an alarm either. I made another mental note to address that deficiency later too.

When I returned from the meter box, she'd been to the loo and was now seated at the old worn cedar table that had been our family's hub for as long as I could remember. What made it different this time was that she had taken my unfinished bottle of sauvignon blanc from the fridge and poured two glasses. The term 'brazen hussy' superseded 'audacious' in my mind; talk about making herself at home! But it made sense if she could raid occupied homes; she already had some of this sort of cheek. Her fearlessness I had to admire. Reluctantly.

Now the light was on I got my first good look at my cat burglar too. Not at all what I had expected. This was no drug addicted street urchin. Instead a pair of the most intelligent and greenest eyes known to mankind answered my shocked gaze. She had a short bob of brown hair and soft lips that seemed to oscillate between indignant anger and bemusement. In another setting this burglar could have passed for a privately educated socialite. To top it off, the black tracksuit I had thought she was wearing now looked more like brushed black velvet – totally fetching. Images of a young Audrey Hepburn flashed before my eyes. Crime was obviously still paying well, especially in this and nearby well-to-do suburbs. And then it clicked; this was no ordinary cat burglar, I'd caught a professional jewel thief, someone who could seamlessly move around high society without raising suspicion. What else could explain the diamond necklace worn effortlessly and without compunction around her neck? This was something my mother cherished with all her heart and would never have let out of her sight. The necklace had been the last remaining gift from Dad when our family had known better times. Glittering with South African diamonds, the necklace represented all the love and short time we'd shared together. After Dad's fatal bout with cancer Mum had done it tough raising my brother and I singlehandedly. Without the life insurance I don't know how we could have gotten through university, let alone kept the family home.

'You've got a cheek, you know, taking that necklace,' I started. 'If only you knew what it means to my mother. Must be worth a bit now, but then you'd know that, wouldn't you? Oh, and the earrings I gave her too. My, you do have good taste.'

The thief seemed initially lost for words, stunned even. Not for long though.

'They're a borrow, I needed them.'

'Listen, Sweetheart,' I said, wondering what words Humphrey Bogart or Clark Gable would have used in this bizarre situation. OK, so I loved old romantic movies, something no one else knew. 'Needing and wanting are not synonymous or mutually exclusive. Do you know what I mean?'

After another sip of wine, she took a long deep breath; I could almost feel her blood pressure rise. It was almost worth it to see her emerald eyes gleam. Talk about sparkling gems. For a moment I wondered what she'd be like in bed. With such a mercurial expression, making love to this thief would be a life-changing experience, if the victim survived the contest, that is. Looking at her reminded me that in some species of spider, the female mates then devours the male, or so I'd heard. What a way to come and go!

'I'll have you know I have a degree in Marketing and Media where a reasonable level of literacy is a pre-requisite. You talk in superfluous redundancies. I take it you know what I mean?'

'Huh, I think it means you're a spoilt brat. Why aren't you working instead of wandering around at night-time stealing from little old ladies?'

Her face was, by now, puce. Even more attractive, but grown darker with rage. I was fascinated. Her eyes now glittered like stars in an outback night sky.

'Listen to me, you sanctimonious, self righteous prick,' she said, prodding my chest, 'No one tells me how to live my life. Certainly not you! If I wanted your useless fucking advice, I would have asked for it.'

The tirade continued. Her invective was nothing short of inspirational. What would she look like naked? Sensational, I answered myself, but with this one it wouldn't matter. She'd felt good enough to eat as is.

'Let me tell you something, 'Sweetheart',' she spat, 'I know your sort.'

'Oh yeah, and what sort is that?' I baited, always wanting to hear what others thought, but not really.

'Chauvinistic pigs who think they're God's gift to women. Well, 'Sweetheart',' she went on scathingly, 'here's one who wouldn't sleep with you if you were the last man on Earth.'

'What makes you think I'd want to sleep with you? Seems to me you're the one bringing this topic up,' I airily countered.

'I've had my offers ...' Her voice suddenly took on a dismissive tone.

'What, on a dark night with a knife to the throat while you take their jewellery?' I posed.

She glowed incandescent. I could have read the newspaper by the intensity; quite revealing and almost amusing really. Apart from her obvious hang-ups on men, I hadn't met such a lively debater, ever. Unbelievably captivating. The angrier she grew, the more appealing; irrational but alluring, oh yeah.

'I'm doing alright.'

'Until now,' I reminded her.

Whilst she was getting her breath back, I refilled our glasses; the dilemma of what to do remained. Surely there was no hurry for the police. Yet. In the kitchen courtroom setting I could be both judge and jury, court in.

'So how do you justify stealing from the rich; financial redistribution or social equalisation?' I proffered.

She snorted. 'No more than your sort. Rich born-to-rule, brown-nosed sorts who charge the earth for doing very little; you should try working yourself for a change.' OK, that hit the target. And hurt. Deeply. So I was expensive, but don't market forces rule?

'Finished?'

'Not even started. I know who you are, I've seen you in the paper. There's more to life than getting your photo taken on every opening night with a different tart.'

'Ah well, that's simply not me,' I croaked, 'I'm ...'

'So denial is not just a river in Egypt.'

I chuckled, and all of this on an empty stomach. Missing the conference meant missing the evening's meal. I needed to refuel.

'Look, until the police arrive, what's say I whip up something?' I said, switching tack to peer inside my mother's fridge.

Seeing the contents, ingredients for a snack but little else, meant extreme culinary imagination was required. My mother never wasted money on food that was for sure. Still, I loved a challenge.

After several minutes and an attack on the second bottle of duty-free wine, it occurred to me I hadn't heard from my captive for a while. A strange sort of silence had descended on the kitchen – I turned my head. Leaning forward in her chair, she was watching me with intense interest. The gaze bordered on fascination, her earlier emotional storm appeared to have passed. Not wanting to spoil the atmosphere, which had turned almost convivial, I slipped half the savoury omelette onto a plate in front of her, a sprig of parsley on top.

'What's this?' she said.

'Despite the circumstances, we still have to eat.' It seemed to me with her nubile figure regular meals were not a high priority, plus she ate as if her last meal had been some time ago.

My eyebrows rose.

'Delicious,' she mumbled, her mouth full of omelette, 'it's what you did with the sautéing the onions, garlic and mushrooms. I wouldn't have thought of that, you can really cook.'

'Oh, so the male does have his purposes,' I said, instantly regretting my words. Sarcasm, my usual defence. For the first time I acknowledged it. 'Sorry.'

'Accepted.'

As I busied myself finding cheese, biscuits and coffee, the insanity of the situation hit me. Was I making a citizen's arrest or not? Shouldn't I be ringing for the police? Or did I have another role to play?

'I don't know your name.'

'Alicia.'

Beautiful name too. 'Alicia, I've been thinking. You've got to change your ways, that's obvious. You need a proper legal job. With your uni qualification that should be straightforward, so ...'

'Wait up,' she interrupted, 'that's not as easy as it sounds ...'

'Bulldust,' I overrode.

'No, if you just listen for a minute. That's something else you do; you talk over people. Let me explain.'

I shrugged my shoulders. Eating humble pie wasn't my strongest suit either.

'All job adverts say experience 'essential', but how can you get the experience without the job? Catch 22.'

'Joseph Heller, 1961,' I stated automatically.

'Exactly, I see myself as a female Yossarian,' she agreed, 'now you understand my dilemma. How do I break that cycle to get a job?'

For long moments her unremitting stare met mine, a battle neither relinquished. In my mind this slip of a girl, or woman really, had everything. Articulate, bright, motivated, good-looking; the world lay in front of her. Why she had gone down the road of theft was beyond me. More lucrative perhaps. Certainly more risky with always the chance of being caught and jail time most likely, or a custodial sentence at the very least. Hmm. Maybe she thrived on burglary's adrenaline rush, who could say?

Then, an idea rose to the surface like a bubble, before bursting into words. Could I turn this misdirected person's life around, a real challenge admittedly, but wouldn't everyone be better off? Rehabilitation! If I could make her see the error of her ways, people could sleep more soundly at night for a start, like my mother upstairs and myself, of course. Could she be a project? Could I point Alicia in another direction? What a thrill and possibly, just possibly, both of us might benefit.

'Alicia,' I started, 'I doubt that you trust me, but do you possess an open mind?'

'I'd like to think so,' she said, a suspicious note in her voice. She was probably wondering if I was going to proposition her, then let her go. Guilty as charged, your Honour, I thought.

'Well, our advertising guy has given his notice and if, this is a big *if*, you can produce the goods, I could put in a word for you. No guarantee. You'd be my apprentice, as it were.' I omitted that the job was in London. 'Oh, and once you've returned the necklace.'

'Over my dead body. Alongside perhaps, but I wouldn't work under you in a million years. I do have some pride left, as you of all people should appreciate.'

I sat back. This wretched thief was amazing. On the shakiest ground ever, she was still trying to dictate terms. Alicia appeared to have sussed me out, exposed my weaknesses and made me take note, things that no female had done before. I wondered if it was because she wanted to be regarded as an equal and not a weak submissive person from the outset.

'Alright, Alicia,' I said, reaching for my mobile phone and playing my trump card, 'then I guess it's the police for you.'

Her hand found itself on top of mine. That's not fair, I thought. A soft, light hand, but one connected to a mind of its own, with a delightful almost seductive touch.

'A month's trial,' she said, 'and I walk away at any time if either of us is unhappy, deal?'

'Deal,' I agreed, trying to turn my hand over so we could shake on it.

All that happened was that our fingers got tangled awkwardly at first, then entwined. As our eyes took in the mess of fingers neither could deny something indefinable was occurring, I knew not what. Had the planets aligned or our brainwaves synchronised, I didn't know, but we had connected. Inexplicable, unbelievable, only time could explain.

Our heads hedged closer together. Alicia, were her lips as kissable as they looked? Emotions overcame logic. The rationality of kissing a thief flew out the window at that moment. Shit, I thought, Graham, you're smitten. Surely a quick kiss wouldn't hurt, would it? With only millimetres separating us, our lips ...

My mother's footsteps creaked on the stairs and the kitchen door opened.

'Ah, Graham, you're back early. Thought I heard voices. I see you've met Alicia, my new boarder. Just come down from Sydney looking for work, haven't you, dear?'

My mouth began to take the appearance of the Luna Park entrance.

'So Alicia, how did your evening go? My old diamonds really suit her, don't you think, Graham? By the way, did you see that your illustrious twin, Bertrand, made it into the paper the other day? I do wish he'd settle down. Still, he's coming around for tea tomorrow night, if the old house electrics don't play up again.'

Now two amazed faces stared aghast at my mother.

'What did I say?' she asked.

Katherine with a K

Chess: A strategic board game designed for two players who battle each other with an army of 16 chess men, the object of which is to keep their king from being checkmated while trying to checkmate the opponent's king. The queen is usually the most powerful piece.

When Katherine (with a K if you don't mind) McInnes won dux of her Year 12 group no one, least of all her parents, was surprised. Wasn't her father, Vice Chancellor of Melbourne University, and her mother, one of Melbourne's leading divorce lawyers, ideal parents for producing a super intelligent child? If only, along with a prodigious brain, Katherine with a K had emotions to suit.

Friendships, especially boyfriends, throughout her schooling were a luxury she could ill afford, a distraction from the essential task of learning. One withering glare from Katherine with a K's icy eyes and any potential admirer slunk away.

Only one fellow student refused to be intimidated. Finally, thwarted to a university scholarship, this courageous lad, possibly emboldened by a dare, 'daked' the school dux on the last day of term. His only reward was the barest glimpse of white cotton briefs before the best right hook ever seen in school history broke his nose. The sharp crack was heard clear across the quadrangle and promptly entered the school annals. Exposed in front of her leering peers Katherine with a K hauled up her track pants before stomping off defiantly to the refuge of the girls' toilets. No longer would his attentive brown eyes follow her every movement around the school. No one bettered this one and got away with it. Absolutely no one.

The end of year school award presentation only brought Katherine with a K a light smatter of applause in keeping with her lack of popularity. No one was surprised either. Her class report read 'very bright but aloof.'

Katherine with a K merged seamlessly into mainstream university life, something not unexpected for a young 17-year-old but more so for an attractive looking girl blessed with an IQ of 172. Dismissing the myriad of social opportunities, the scholarship winner applied herself to study with an almost religious fervour that would have put Einstein to shame. Even the uni MENSA group aroused no interest. 'Boring,' she'd said. 'Where's the challenge in that?'

'I think you'll find that particular reaction is exothermic rather than endothermic,' she corrected one of her lecturers during his lecture.

Taking a second look over his glasses at the audience, he made a correction in his notes. Sharp as a knife, but blunt as a hammer, was his impression of this top student.

Just as nature had endowed this student with superlative intellect, it had not left her looks far behind. A flick of mousy brown hair masked ice cool blue eyes that topped a lithe body, one that most males longed to get closer to and see more of. As repelling all borders became second nature, her reputation as 'ice queen' increased the odds of bedding such a desirable student to 500:1. Not that anyone ever collected. Her fellow female students soon learnt to ignore her while even the most tenacious and ardent male suitor eventually gave up.

Katherine with a K's one concession to a social outlet was a fascination, some thought closer to manic obsession, with the game of chess. Leading the university's chess team, she rapidly propelled the institution through a win at National level, her father being particularly proud. He had introduced her to the game, while her feminist mother honed her daughter's killer instincts to razor sharpness? Surely destroying opposition on a chessboard was mere child's play for her, no one could better her strategies and no one could better her.

When Katherine with a K transferred to the other side of the scholastic desk as a lecturer with a PhD a few years later, still no one was surprised. Didn't a professional academic life perfectly suit someone so focussed on intellectual goals? Sporting a work ethic that left other academic staff in awe, she fitted into university life like fingers in a winter woollen glove. For a moment she reflected. Youngest lecturer in a predominantly male domain, what else did the future hold? Certainly she wasn't wasting her superior intellect on frivolous love or on bearing dirty, noisy and smelly children.

'Visitors are not encouraged to distract staff, Suzanne,' admonished Katherine with a K, her ice blue eyes raking over the lanky guy leaning over the faculty secretary's desk. She added an aside, 'Ah, I see your nose has healed reasonably well.'

Saying farewell and kissing Suzanne's forehead, the visitor bit his lip, cast a fleeting look around the office and left quietly, heading to the tram stop outside the Chemical Engineering faculty. Again he had learnt his place in her world. No one had beaten Katherine with a K. Yet.

It was Katherine with a K's practice to keep a large chess set in her office and, due to the lack of suitable opponents, she played both sides, alternately pitting herself against herself in a ruthless pursuit of perfection. Fickle emotion had no place in strategy. Chess was her one all encompassing passion, the science of the interacting moves engaging her every thought. Grandmaster one day, why not?

'Who's been in my office?' she demanded of the faculty secretary. 'Well?'

'No one, to my knowledge Ms McInnes,' came the answer, 'Except myself, of course.'

'Hmm,' reflected Katherine with a K.

Not by chance had she noticed that a white pawn had been moved on her office board, something she instinctively recognised as an unusual first move. 1.e4 e5. Before leaving she casually responded. 2.Nf3d6.

But again the following day, another move appeared. 3.d4 Bg4. No, surely it couldn't be a possible beginning of the Kasparov Stratagem IV, something never before witnessed outside any Eastern bloc countries. Wasn't Russia considered the home of chess, a country renown for producing the world's best male players of chess? Why hadn't she been born in a country that revered chess as a national pastime and an Olympic sport? Should she employ a famous opening, gambit, defence or even develop one of her own? How could this game be happening right under her pert nose? Could she be the first Western woman to take on and defeat such a male opponent? Her tinder of imagination was ignited, transformed into a bush fire and burnt wildly. 4.dxe5 Bxf3.

Here level of interest in the game being played out in her office rose. Obviously someone was playing against her, but who? With all the university staff and students already accounted for, Katherine with a K reasoned it had to be someone with access to her office outside class hours. Could it possibly be a migrant Ukrainian cleaner; the identity of her opponent caused oscillations between great intrigue and frustration. Even alerting the security staff to the potential presence of an intruder drew no response. At every step her investigations were stymied. He was invisible to the CCTV cameras. The mystery continued. 5.Qxf3 dxe5.

Each day brought a new move. Each day her imagination grew, a new experience for this emotionally virginal brain. By the end of the second week Katherine with a K realised that her night-time opponent was a formidable adversary. The moves were purely tactical, forcing her to use every brain cell to combat the ruthless game being played out against her. The pile of her lost pieces grew. Everything, she knew, was at risk. Who was he? Two more things were obvious: she could hardly wait for the morning to discover the latest overnight move and, for the first time in her life, her fingers tingled when she removed the opponent's chess pieces. Despite everything, she knew sacrifices of pieces often had to be made, hopefully of lesser value, to secure a strategic advantage over the opposition, the end goal being to checkmate the king. 6.Bc4 Nf6. This game was no different. Lost pieces from both players littered each end of the board.

Failing to identify her opponent, she tried to concentrate her energy on beating the person behind the moves. If only her mind wouldn't keep wondering who was audacious enough to penetrate the university security and challenge her very rationality. Balancing chemical equations, yes, somewhere where equations of the heart existed, no. Logic, always, emotions, never. But this time her feelings as well were under siege. Strangely she felt alive, engaged. Who was he? What did he really want with her? 7.Qb3 Qe7.

'Is everything alright, Ms McInnes?' the secretary inquired as Katherine with a K whisked past her office that morning. A dismissive wave was her reply. 8.Nc3 c6.

This particular morning was different. With only minutes to go before her lecture began she noticed the corner of a note under the chess board. The note read, 'Surrender?' Katherine with a K's eyes widened. Would she soon discover the identity of the mystery player? The game was now at a crucial stage, what should she do? Pressure mounted. 9.Bg5 b5.

Leaning back in her leather office chair she hurriedly considered her options, the ones on the board and the ones in her life. More than chess was at stake. Focus, if only she could.

Her note in reply read, 'In your dreams.' 10.Nxb5 cxb5.

Maybe a reprieve existed. 11.Bxb5+ Nbd7.

'Who are you?' read her note. 12.0-0-0 Rd8.

'Beat me first.' Katherine with a K's eyes narrowed and grew more determined. 13.Rxd7 Rxd7.

'Not your best move. Dinner one night perhaps?' was his following invitation.

Katherine with a K smarted at the message. Her as a human prize, never, but on the other hand an inner voice long dormant for 28 years said the opposite. 'Maybe,' she wrote. Anonymous, discrete, exciting, all in the unlikely case she lost the game.

His next note read,' Let's make the game a little more interesting, fancy a wager?' 14.Rd1 Qe6.

'You'll never win, but what do you want?' she wrote. 15.Bxd7+ Nxd7.

'You!' he wrote back, 'Agreed? In the unlikely case I win, of course.' 16.Qb8+ Nxb8.

Her bottom jaw fell like her track pants had years before. Katherine gasped, her face blushing as blood coursed through her body like a flood. For a moment all reason left her head and long fingers shook over her king piece. Of course, she thought, he had inveigled his way into her life, his one ambition to mentally seduce her. Could he be a stalker? How had she let this happen? Why had her brain responded in such a crazy way; her thoughts wandering around every topic but the essential moves. Curiosity overtook logic. Was he old, was he young? What did he think of her? Concentrate. The game grew tense; she sensed the end was near.

Their last night was their first. 17.Rd8, check?

Katherine with a K poured over the board. For once she was at the mercy of an unknown. Her black king was under threat from a rook alongside and a bishop protecting from outside. Checkmate. No moves available. But she could hardly leave with herself in such a position. Maybe she should ask for more time or did she just want to meet her mystery player? How had she let this psychological weakness take control? This Katherine with a K had played like a child, what must he think of her?

A knock came against her door. 'Night, Ms McInnes,' the secretary intoned. 'Want a lift home?'

'No, I don't think so, Suzanne. Thank you anyway.'

Giving a long drawn out sigh, Katherine with a K saw all her life run before her. OK, the position was untenable. She lowered her black king onto its side in surrender. Truth hurt, she had been beaten in a child's game. Could there be other games to play, more to learn about life and all its mysteries? Now, how would her opponent appear? How would he claim his victory? Who was he? What did he really want from her? Into her chair she sagged, defeated.

'Waiting for anyone?' her secretary persisted, leaning into the office.

'No, there's no one.' Suddenly Katherine with a K saw her life for what it was, empty. A modern minimalist flat, only a bike with a flat tyre to share her bedroom and a faithless cat roaming the streets at night. Hardly worth going home for. Hadn't she lost at everything?

'A knight on a white horse perhaps?' Suzanne posed, holding up the chess piece, then grinned.

With a start Katherine with a K straightened, her body rigid in shock. How did Suzanne know about this game? No way could it be her, or was she a pawn in a bigger game? Her eyebrows knitted in thought.

'You don't remember me from school, do you?' Her secretary's question was more like a statement. 'I was only in Year 7 when you got dacked and king-hit Antoine. Talk of the school.' Another grin lit her face.

A wry smile grew on Katherine with a K's lips as she reminisced.

'Everyone knows it,' Suzanne high fived her, 'you two are so right for one another. Stop denying your feelings. My brother is smart, don't you think? Should have seen the look on your face each day, absolutely priceless. Now come on, grab your bag. With luck we won't be late. It's his turn to make tea. Antoine's always had the hots for you but don't tell him I said so.'

'But ...' Bloody Antoine. And yet hadn't it seemed strangely flattering that his eyes always followed her around the schoolyard all those years ago? Last she'd heard he was a construction engineer and divorced after catching his wife flagrante delicto. Antoine, of course, hmm.

'No buts. Now put down that laptop and come on,' Suzanne persisted.

'I'm not really dressed to go out,' protested Katherine with a K.

'You look fine, Ms McInnes. And you can crash on the sofa tonight if you want to.'

'How did you do it?'

A laugh escaped Suzanne. 'A glass of wine first. Antoine always said "Bulldust baffles brains." Heaven only knows he's full of it.'

The two women looked at one another. Katherine with a K glanced down at Suzanne's mobile phone and rapidly developed a hypothesis. Complicit with her secretary at the end of that phone her adversary existed, armed with Internet connection. Oh no, had she been playing a computer? With the best websites available she had been unwittingly playing the entire world. No wonder she had lost. So there was a conspiracy of love against her after all. A silent moan escaped as she prepared to confront her destiny.

First she would face her high school nemesis. Yet again. OK, he'd got her attention, now to find whether the man matched his charisma.

'Call me Katherine ...'

'OK, Katherine.' Suzanne smiled.

' ... with a K.'

How to
Have the Ideal Family

An ideal family, Papa said, should be self sufficient, something my parents practised using their small Northern Italian village talents. Everyone should contribute to the family through their unique skills, the ideal family being able to survive without money changing hands. Trading was an art form, he said.

Little for Papa when he immigrating to Australia in the 70's. From laying concrete in Italy he began laying concrete in the northern Melbourne suburb of Brunswick. His was an 'arranged' marriage. Before they left Belluno, Mama 'arranged' to marry Papa by falling pregnant with my eldest brother, Angelo. I arrived 20 years later, the youngest and last of six kids. It was understood from an early age that with we were expected to contribute to the family using our unique God-given skills. No one was exempt. No one, not even in-laws.

No one could mistake our house. Two white concrete lions adorned the widest concrete 'driveway' that surrounded our grandiose white rendered two-storey house. Despite huge concrete columns adorning the front portico, everyone came around the back following the sweet cooking aromas coming from Mama's kitchen. That's the way it was at our place. At the rear was a huge undercover area complete with pizza oven and grape vines along the back fence. More like an airport, not a single blade of grass was game to raise its head in the concrete jungle outside.

No one could mistake our heritage either. Our school lunch, strangely enough rarely envied, consisted of rough salami, cheese and crusty bread, pickled onions, seasonal fruit and, if we were lucky, a couple of olives. Occasionally Mama snuck in a cold boiled egg as a treat. Few fought to sit next to us in the classroom after lunch!

Angelo was a bricklayer so he built everyone's houses. After a whirlwind courtship he married Tracy, a talented dressmaker who used her magical fingers to make the best fashions ever. Second brother, Ricardo, was an electrician and lived with Simone, a book-keeper who was not yet married or pregnant, much to Mama's concern. Third brother Alfonso was the family joker but a great plumber according to everyone. No one's pipes leaked when he was around. His wife, Maria was a 'verra gooda' cook, something even my plump Mama admitted to. Rare praise, indeed. For vegetables the family relied on brother number four, Carlo, who ran a greengrocer's shop and was inseparable from his wife Marie, even at work. Carmelo, their 3-year-old usually ran nappy-less up and down the aisles. Whilst the spouses' names caused confusion, no one minded after a glass or two of Uncle Dominic's home-made wine. I suspected Uncle Dom of being secretly gay, but Mama said he had just been unlucky in love. As if! Last brother and butcher, Roberto, had a reputation for the best Italian sausages around. In June he'd married his assistant, Silvia, after a passionate affair conducted in the cool room. I recalled she was due around Christmas time. Hmm. Uncle Jimmy was my Mama's brother and a good one to avoid when he had been drinking. A confirmed bachelor with overly wandering hands, if you know what I mean. On my father's side Uncle Pat was a house painter, a frustrated Michelangelo apparently, his mantra was 'cash was king.' His wife, Aunty Sophia, was an amazing person, combining house rendering and plastering; but sculpture was her real passion. From the 'interesting' pieces of art on their walls I wondered if they modelled for one another. Too much information.

Family gatherings at our place became an instant party; kids ran around everywhere. Much shouting, drinking and hilarity abounded where we laughed, yelled, fought and made up, all on the same night. Contrary to appearances, unconditional family love ruled.

As only daughter, my position in the family was tricky. Caught between two cultures, Italian and Australian, I wanted my independence. At the same time my parents watched my every movement with grave concern. The family honour was apparently at stake. Any guy I showed the slightest interest in had soon been given short shrift. Amazingly this issue had never arisen with my brothers who had been encouraged to go out and sow their wild oats with any willing Aussie girl. How gross.

The shrill scream of the police siren seemingly right next to my ear scared the living daylights out of me. All because of a little U-turn, a minute's driving indiscretion at the most, what an overreaction all this fuss was. Did they really need to have all those embarrassing lights flashing? Especially outside my client's house.

No problems I thought, hiking my short dress up and adjusting my top down to daring depths as the cop strode over. Well rehearsed, this ploy had worked perfectly before. What male could resist this visually overwhelming feast?

'Sorry, Officer,' I grovelled, flashing my teeth, straightened by dentist Uncle Dom after Papa had concreted his entire backyard. Weird, the cop's eyes never left mine.

'$50 and two demerit points,' he said, 'Licence?' Then I twigged, OK, this guy wanted my personal details for later so I added my business card. Mobile hairdresser, all cash, no tax, a trade Papa approved of wholeheartedly. Not that my father's shiny bald head had much need of my hairdressing ministrations in our ideal family. Too much testosterone, he'd said with a knowing grin.

'Failure to display P plates too,' the cop mumbled, scribbling away before thrusting the ticket along with my card back through the window. In the background I could see his work partner on her mobile phone inside the patrol car, quite oblivious to my dire situation. What made it worse was that I'd gone to school with Kirrily; she would have let me off for sure, instead of this stone-faced road bully.

'Watch out you don't catch a chill now,' he said grinning in an aside. Was that a chuckle too?

In absolute disgust I took off abruptly, the cop had to step back rapidly to avoid his foot being run over. Serve him right, I thought. Bloody smart arse.

As luck would have it, my hairdryer fused one Friday making me late for every afternoon appointment. Whilst speeding along with my radio up loud, hoping to catch up the lost time, I hardly noticed the bright, flashing lights behind until too late.

'Going to a fire are we? It's 50 in local streets, $50 and another two demerit points,' the now familiar voice growled at my window. Inwardly I fumed and automatically held out my hand for the ticket. Didn't he know how hard I worked at my job? Being mobile meant travel time ate into the day. It wasn't easy juggling appointments let alone keeping all the oldies happy with perms and colours. They all expected discounts, meaning I had to inflate my charges beforehand to make a decent living. In the ideal family, of course, members got free treatments.

The final straw came later that night. Last appointment.

As I piled my gear into the back seat, a bulbous flat tyre looked up at me as black rain clouds loomed. Latent feelings took over, black mascara tears ran down my cheeks. It had been my worst day, now this, another expense. Could it get any worse? I kicked the dratted tyre with all my might, just as the gaudily striped and checked car pulled alongside. Again. Along with my pride, my toes now hurt.

'What now?' I sobbed. Was he going to charge me with obstructing a footpath or something?

'Need a hand? It's OK, Ms Grilli. I'm off-duty.'

I shrugged my shoulders. Uncle Jimmy, Papa's brother-in-law, did all the family's car repairs leaving me clueless. Putting petrol in was the limit of my automotive knowledge, even that proved tricky at times. All the same, this was seriously strange. This crazy cop, first he fined me, then he wanted to help me, where was he coming from? On the other hand, there was something about a man in uniform, especially this tall, brown-eyed Adonis. OK, so the light was bad.

As we both bumbled about trying to change the wheel, I learnt it was his first week on patrol. He was sorry about my case, there was a quota of bookings to be met. He was still learning the ropes, which way did the wheel nuts go and would I like to have a drink one night? Dropping a nut down the drain, I giggled, he laughed, our eyes met again, we kissed and that was it.

Fast forward six months.

My relationship with the cop, Andrew, was like a budding flower about to burst into full bloom. Seriously in love, we could hardly keep our hands off one another during our weekly clandestine meetings behind the police station whilst I was meant to be doing Tracy's blonde tips. The moment we looked into each other's eyes an exquisite shiver ran down my spine, my cop said he felt the same. Andrew was like no other, but what to do? To add to a sense of desperation there remained only one obstacle, Papa, and to a lesser extent, Mama.

Even aged 21 I knew my love interest characterized all that was wrong with Papa's adopted homeland. Andrew was deemed professional, incorruptible, represented authority and did not deal in cash. Useless with his hands, no tradesman was he. What good would this cop be to the ideal family? Not only that, he could pose a threat to the family's nefarious paperless and tax-less 'operations'. I had to face it, Papa would never accept a cop for a son-in-law while his fat bum pointed to the ground. So there our relationship stood, unconsummated and in limbo; Papa would have killed anyone who 'touched' me before marriage, whilst I would have killed anyone who didn't at least try!

Frustration ruled.

It seemed ours was to be an unrequited love; parental approval, something not forthcoming, was needed for our love to flourish. Just ring if anything changes, I'll be there in a flash, were Andrew's final words to me. We promised eternal love, kissed for the last time and parted ways, swearing if we somehow met again we'd pretend not to recognise one another. It would just make life so much more difficult if we did.

I despaired.

Hope came from a strange direction.

Our house was robbed! But not just robbed, rather a very selective robbery occurred where the thief took advantage of a rare opportunity when the house was empty. The robbery changed everything. Along with the biggest flat screen TV that money could buy, wads of cash were stolen from under the matrimonial bed. Papa nearly collapsed in shock. For a while I was very worried how he would cope with the trauma. Much worse though, the treasure of his life was also taken; a gold filigree cameo brooch allegedly from his great, great grandmother who'd had a 'castle' in Belluno. She had been a Countess, he said, and a confidant of the Pope. The brooch meant everything to Papa, more than it did to Mama or any of us kids; it represented his origins. He was devastated by the loss. Completely and absolutely devastated beyond belief.

What did I do about the robbery? I rang for the police.

It seemed no time before Constable Andrew Newsom arrived at the crime scene; he quickly took charge, wrote copious notes and meticulously inspected every window and door for signs of forced entry. Strangely there were none. So impressed with this professional police approach, I made coffee for us all. In Mama's pantry was some nice home-made panettone too.

Before the cop left, my father extracted a promise that no stone was left unturned for the return of the brooch, he even hinted at a cash reward.

'Mr Grilli, this case will have my undivided attention. Rest assured the thief will not evade justice.'

'Justa get the Countess' brooch back, that's all I ask,' Papa said, waving his hands in supplication.

Over the next months Andrew dropped in each week with an update on the break-in. First of all he managed to return the stolen TV; a month or so later he asked Papa to identify an old leather satchel of used bank notes.

'Can you identify the money, Mr Grilli?'

'Isa right bag,' Papa said.

'Maybe we should count the money,' Andrew suggested, 'although I'll overlook the need for a receipt just this time.'

'Looksa OK to me, dona worry 'bout it. You finda da brooch?'

'No, Mr Grilli, but we're getting closer. I'm sure of it.'

'May as well stay for tea, Constable,' I chipped in. 'Is that OK, Papa?'

'Sure thing, Angela. He's too skinny for a cop anyway, isn't he Papa?' said Mama.

Having two phones in the house was sometimes a curse, sometimes a blessing. This time, instead of others thwarting my personal life, it meant I could overhear the conversation.

'Ah, Mr Grilli, Constable Newsom of Brunswick Police here.'

'So Andrea, you finda da brooch?' an air of hope rose in Papa's voice.

'As a matter of fact, I might have,' Andrew said.

'You wanta for mea to come to da station?'

'No, no, that won't be necessary, maybe I can drop in?'

'Heh, of course, of course.'

'Mr Grilli, I have to warn you, there may be expenses involved in the brooch's recovery.'

'Dona worry 'bout a ting. I can paya cash.'

No one had ever seen my father so emotional. Tears ran down his cheeks when Andrew carefully unwrapped the precious brooch and placed it in Papa's hand; he hugged the cop like there was no tomorrow.

'Did I tell you this was my great, great grandmamma's, a countess, no less? Eh, Momma, the polizia never this good-a-back in the old country, eh? Maybe you bitta Italiano?'

Andrew smiled.

'And you always welcome in our home, Andrea, you hear this?'

'Now down to business, Mr Grilli, the cost.'

'No problema, you say how mucha,' Papa said reaching around for his thick cash-swollen wallet.

'I'd like to take your daughter, Angela, out, Mr Grilli, if she doesn't mind, that is.'

'Sure, sure,' my father, now sensing a financial bargain, yelled out to me in the kitchen, 'Hey, Angela there's someone here to see you. Be vera nice to him, OK? He-a-friend of the family now.'

Papa wrapped his arms around Andrew's shoulders. 'Who else you know hassa great, great grandmamma a countess, a clossa friend of the Pope's as wella? Eh?'

'You have an amazing family, Mr Grilli, such a beautiful daughter too. In fact, it's an ideal family, you should be very proud.'

Papa's chest puffed out so much I wondered if his already strained shirt buttons were going to pop.

As we headed outside out of sight, Andrew gave me a passionate, seriously-long-overdue kiss, surreptitiously passing our front door key back into my hand. I put my arm in his and welcomed him into the ideal family.

A Sorrento Tradie
and a Ring Top

Coming home from overseas can be quite a letdown. A late night flight arrival and jet lag doesn't help. After travelling so far to experience the best the world supposedly has to offer, and finding it only marginally different to home, can be quite disconcerting. Anyone who's compared the congested roads overseas to stationary Ocean Beach Road summer traffic will agree. But how can a quarry be thinly disguised as an English beach? Our sandy shallow Port Phillip Bay with aquamarine waters can mix it with the world's best, even discounting the Channel dredging and E coli levels from Rosebud dog poo. Still, I hoped the new desalination plant wouldn't dry up our Bay. And didn't my home town of Sorrento have the best women's clothing shops on the Peninsula? Trendy hairdressers' too. What else could one possibly need?

As the opening of my rented flat's front door cut a swath through a month's accumulation of bills and junk mail strewn across the floor, I was reminded that I was broke - desperate too. In reality the surplus of handsome Latin males in Europe turned out to be another myth, more like a bevy of swarthy egotists with overly wandering hands.

But now reality set in. I crammed the smelliest clothes into my parents' cast-off prehistoric washing machine, one with knobs, not touch-panel, cranked up the hand-me-down stereo and plugged in my trusty, rusty electric bar heater, probably the last electrical appliance to be made in Australia. Two huge coils ran in front of a moulding of a real wood fire; it even looked warm when off. The heater was one of my favourite finds during a nature strip rubbish collection, only requiring a hairpin in the fuse holder to create a cosy ambience rarely experienced these days. Why was it so cold here despite global warming?

I flicked the switch.

Imagine my surprise when all the might of the once great Latrobe Valley electricity suddenly faded, leaving me quite alone in dark and in deathly silence. What to do?

Then I had a brainwave. Peering through my darkened curtains, I wondered if the guy next door might possibly prove useful. Why else would there be a tradie's Ute parked outside, prominent stickers on his back window proclaiming, 'Footscray for Premiers' and 'Put a spark in your life, marry an electrician.' As if! Surely the sea breezes were not sufficiently strong to require through bolts to hold the surfboard onto his roof rack. Very curious that.

To give my neighbour his due, he eventually answered the door, if only a little sleepily at two o'clock in the morning.

Where was his compassion for a fellow human being in crisis? Was it my fault he had to start work so early? At least, once he woke up more, he had a friendly manner. Needing a shave but with peroxide-bleached blonde hair, the palest pair of blue eyes, gaping stubbies and a holey singlet, I was singularly impressed. Who wouldn't be?

After agreeing to help me out, my key role in fixing the errant fuse was to hold up the heavy meter box lid while he poked around underneath, muttering some foreign gibberish that included strange words like 'amps and whatses'. Although we women are meant to be good at multi tasking, he expected me to hold the torch as well. I mean, really! And I don't think I should be blamed for letting the lid fall on his head. How was I to know that the daddy long legs crawling up my calf wasn't poisonous, unlike the look my neighbour gave me in the torchlight as he rubbed the back of his bruised head? Weren't men meant to be tough? Just look at the Collingwood AFL footballers, no sense, no feeling. What other team required a second try to win the Grand Final? I rest my case!

And if my 'sparky' neighbour got glimpses of my silhouette through the pure silk pyjamas against the torch beam, strangely this time I didn't mind his somewhat attentive gaze. Amazing what comes out a silk worm's bum though, isn't it?

'Of course, I've seen you in the distance. Meant to say hello before you went away,' he said.

'Oh, right.' How could I tell him I had only gone out with professional guys in leased convertibles? Could I somehow compare my neighbour's work Ute with my mother's menopausal mauve Mazda MX5? Hmm.

'Must have a drink sometime soon. Now, you look cold and I've got to get up early. 'Night.'

I glanced down to see two Eiffel Tower tall nipples pressing against my pyjama top.

'Oh my God.'

At that point I gave Evan, we were now on first name basis, a quick thank you peck on the cheek and left him standing there looking quite bemused, or possibly a bit stunned.

We returned to our respective beds. I fell asleep immediately, quite worn out with the stress of complex electrical repairs and all the excitement in my meter box. It had been a very thought-provoking experience.

The next day I caught the 788 bus along Nepean Road to see my maternal parent and self-appointed life coach.

My mother, never to be called mum or mom to her face, obviously had special insight. Always look to the future, she advised, the benefits of an expensive Toorak College education coming to the fore. Apparently a university degree was essential in a man. Money counted. Not by accident did she have the most watertight pre-nuptial agreement with my father and, apart from me, this was her finest achievement. Didn't stop him straying though. Still, now she lived in nearby elite Portsea and he in working-class Altona. So who won? My mother had the grandest mansion, where everything worked. Whenever anything needed fixing, she got a tradesman in straightaway, no expense spared. Cosmetic surgery was her hobby, need I say more?

In contrast, my dad always spoke wistfully about an old favourite haunt, the Dromana Drive-in, saying it was very family friendly. Then he usually looked wistfully at me, saying that's where maybe he'd started our family, meaning yours truly. Yuck! Too much information!

But for me the usual third degree began.

'Well, Amanda? What about that medical student you were seeing?' she demanded.

'Always wanted me to dress up in nurses' uniforms, mother, and practise breast examinations.'

'Oh dear. And that accountant?'

'Only interested in my figure.'

'That solicitor fellow?'

'Just wanted to sleep with me.'

'I don't know what the world's coming to, dear,' she paused for thought. 'Now what about that Collins Street specialist, he was quite cute I thought. If I was a year or two younger myself ...'

'The gynaecologist? He only wanted to look at my ...'

'Never mind, Amanda,' she hastily went on. 'I'm sure you'll find someone suitable one day. Go blonde like me. And don't forget that biological clock of yours is ticking. Don't want your eggs to get hard-boiled.'

For some reason my mother never mentioned tradies as a viable option.

'You can start in two weeks, but no more lap work, alright,' my old boss chortled. Yippee!

I had crawled back to my old waitressing job at the local Continental Hotel. There they had the heaviest crockery, always slipping out of my hands at the worst possible times. My old nickname of 'Lap Dancer' was grossly unfair. After all, I had hoped the boss had forgotten the incident of me pouring a schooner of beer on some fat guy's lap; he should never have pinched my bum in the first place. Said he was just getting his hanky out! How was I expected to know he was the hotel owner? At the time, in one fell swoop, I won a round of applause swiftly followed by the sack.

But seeing I was short of the readies, a quick trip down to the nearby Blairgowrie Op Shop followed. This always resulted in cheap glam wear. This was where my mother discarded her designer clothes and I surreptitiously bought them back for a song. If it was good enough for her ...

'Darling, you must be doing well,' she said whilst having coffee a couple of days later. 'Did some man give it to you? I had a dress just like that. Too expensive for you, though.'

So I murmured cattily almost too softly for her to hear, 'But at least I can get into it without looking like a Michelin man.' Neither did I want to end up frozen-faced like her with injections of salmonella or whatever poison was fashionable that week. As for silicone implants, at least all I had up top was my own. No spastic surgeon was going to grope me under the influence of anaesthetic. Too risky anyway. A while back my second-best friend's breast enhancement surgery went terribly wrong when one of her implanted boobs drooped. She blamed her amorous boyfriend who claimed to be the breaststroke champion at the Athenæum, - the old Sorrento picture theatre, that is. They were a well suited couple; he was a bit cockeyed, she was now cocktitted.

But I digress.

'Have you met someone? You look flushed, or is it hormones?' my mother quizzed mercilessly.

'Just the guy next door. Apparently he's self employed. A tradie. Owns his own place too. He's different, cute, works hard, I wonder whether ...'

'Not a plumber is he? I need someone to clear out my drains. They always work better when I have a good flush with a power plunger every now and then. My house cleaner says she has a live-in tradie plumber in her husband. Apparently very good with his hands, saves an absolute fortune and always on call. Won't give me his name though, funny that.'

I left feeling more confused than before.

The following week my next crisis came when an unwanted suitor from a previous life made very uncharacteristic advances to me in the kitchen, and before main course too! Apparently he misinterpreted my low cut top as an invitation to touch the merchandise. Fortunately my reputation, and virtue, was saved by the screech of my cooking timer, that some may know as a smoke alarm. Leaving the roast chicken to burn more than it already was, I bolted out the back door. My plan was to vault the low side fence and hide there, just as I'd done successfully before. Was it my fault that some fool had newly planted a rose bush right on my usual escape path? Absolutely not! However the pain of thorns scratching their way up my bare legs didn't detract from my muted cries for help. Any movement was excruciating. It seemed as though all my hopes of child bearing were at risk. No prick had ever got so close to the baby factory. Of course, hadn't my horoscope advised me to 'embrace thorny issues and prepare for change?' Yes, now I knew, this was my 'Eureka' moment.

Luckily my handy handsome neighbour-rescuer appeared, having heard my cries. He turned out to be amazingly imaginative. Using his tradie's ladder, he leant over and plucked me right out of that cruel rose bush like a cork from a bottle. I only screamed a little. And was it my fault that the ladder sagged in the sandy soil and over we toppled? I think not! How very unfortunate that it delivered another blow to his forehead and ego. Just as I'd imagined, the relief to be found in his muscular arms was bliss, sheer bliss. At least his disposition improved markedly when I gave him another peck on his cheek (on the unbruised side), to say thanks. I couldn't see his expression in the dark but I'm sure he appreciated this heartfelt gesture. His sweet and prolonged return kiss on my lips proved it. Wow! During this stage, lying on the ground next to him, albeit somewhat winded, I began to seriously question my mother's advice. My rescuer and I could have both been concussed, but I swore we felt strongly connected in some way, or it might have been just his tool belt of screwdrivers and pliers that were somehow caught up in my dress.

After checking the coast was clear of unwanted suitors in my flat, I invited my brave rescuer and tradie neighbour inside. The very least I could do was to clean off the blood from where the ladder had viciously struck him. Why were ladders built with such sharp edges I wondered? Still, what good fortune I had ducked at that moment. Maybe he now saw me in a new light; I've heard concussion can do that to you.

As we chatted, I tipsily sipped my chilled Cups Estate chardonnay, while on the other side of the kitchen table my neighbour cracked open a can of beer. To his credit, his hand skills with a cotton bud had proven exemplary and totally trustworthy. At least the mercurochrome on his cut wasn't too obvious, unlike my orange striped legs. I could have doubled as a tiger from the Melbourne Zoo!

'You know, Evan, I've always had a soft spot for life savers. I don't suppose you ever went to university?' Could he meet my mother's essential criteria? Dare I hope? Maybe, maybe not.

Then I got the surprise of my life. My heart leapt at his words.

'As a matter of fact, I have, Mandy,' Inside I cheered. Yes! Mother would be thrilled and my future assured.

'Yup, went to Monash Uni on a cabling job just a few months back. Had to rewire a chem lab. Tricky job, but still made a packet though. Might buy a decent work trailer now.'

Blast! I groaned but persisted. Should I give him marks for trying? Or should I just pray for him to be a romantic, like me?

'Evan, hypothetically speaking, if someone was supposedly attracted to you, and you were attracted to them, what's the most romantic gesture you could think of? Something that would keep a woman captivated and breathless for a lifetime?'

That was when, without hesitation, he noisily cracked open another can of beer. Inwardly I cringed. At least I had tried. Pity. Was the moment lost forever? Then he leaned forward with the ring top between his fingers in front of us. Reaching for my left hand, he looked me unflinchingly in the eyes. Such lovable blue eyes, honest eyes, tradesman's eyes. Evan gently held my third finger and poised the ring top at the tip. For a moment the world stood still.

'If this fits, Cinderella, can I be your Prince Charming? What do ya reckon?'

My breath stopped. My hand trembled. My heart thumped madly. I very nearly swooned on the spot. How did he know that the old fable of Cinderella was my ever-present fantasy? At that precise instant I fell in love, it was that fast, my epiphany was complete.

And how would I explain my Foster's ring top engagement ring to my mother? I no longer cared.

A Cure for Writer's Block

When I heard from the postie that my next-door neighbour was a retired newspaper journalist (an 'old hack' was the exact description used), it seemed like too good an opportunity to ignore. Staring at the computer screen for hours had elicited nothing. Endless cups of coffee and walks down the rose-scented streets had conjured up nothing except inflamed sinuses. I had writer's block, a constipation of the mind; nothing seemed to shift the malaise in my brain. No words spilled forth; maybe my creativity had run its distance. Plenty of perspiration but no inspiration. My job as an online editor was never at threat but maybe my career as a writer was over before it had begun. I was sick of editing others' work when maybe I could be creating my own stories instead. Maybe, maybe, maybe nothing.

What I needed was a mental laxative to purge the clogged knot of verbiage backlogged in my mind. Something had gone wrong between the grey matter and my right hand. Writer's block, ah!

My only hope rested in gaining some inspiration from my neighbour. An experienced, professional journalist was sure to know exactly what to do, like a mechanic can fix a flat tyre. In him I placed all my trust and hope.

I knocked. Eventually he answered. Hallelujah, salvation at last.

'What do you want?' he demanded, as a set of rheumy eyes looked right past me. Oh shit, so he was blind, exactly what I needed. The postie hadn't mentioned that detail. Strange accent too. Slavic?

'I, I, I just wanted to say hello,' I stammered, leaning back at his latent intensity. 'I saw you were home, so ...' I paused, deciding truth might provide a better alternative. 'OK, I need a favour, I need someone to read my manuscript and give me some hints. Writer's block, so it's a bit unfinished.'

His eyes flickered over me somewhat superficially, at any moment I expected the front door to slam in my face. What could he see anyway?

'I can't read it ...' he said, his hands raised in supplication.

'OK, sorry to have troubled you,' I said and went to turn away.

'But you can read it to me ...' he said, reaching out to pull me inside. I felt like a hapless victim being dragged in for verbal slaughter. 'Come in. Your voice says to me that you can be trusted. Watch where you step, the place is a mess. Don't touch anything.'

I followed his hesitant pattering steps down the dingy hallway, his hands brushing the walls until the lounge opening came up. He appeared to navigate the furniture as if a well worn path was burnt into his brain and plonked himself down with a drawn-out sigh in a threadbare chair next to the window. The afternoon light streamed in, highlighting his wrinkled skin that was gnarled like an old tree trunk. This, along with a prominent magpie's nose, showed his was a face that had seen a lot of life. If I hadn't known he was a journalist I would have said he had spent most of his time outdoors. His age I guessed as being in the eighties. For a moment I wondered what use he could possibly be to me. Had I made a terrible mistake? Was I there under false pretences?

'Well now, my dear, I take it you can operate a kettle?' a wistful smile accompanied his unmistaken hint. 'Milk and plenty of sugar. There might even be an old biscuit in the pantry if you want.'

So began my first attempt at removing my writer's block.

With my new mentor just next door, I found myself visiting most days, sometimes bearing some leftovers, sometimes not. At home, I ate most meals standing up, spooning straight from the tin, but with the prospect of freeing myself from the accursed writer's block I wondered whether eating an occasional sit down meal next door was a better prospect.

'Hello, Mr Saporiski, I mean Pieter, it's just me.'

'Who?' a tremulous voice came from the bowels of his house far away.

'Sophie from next door,' I yelled, pushed at the door and going in.

But it wasn't my neighbour who stood in the doorway, not unless he'd lost 50 kilos and gained six inches overnight. And then it clicked. The small white car with the door emblem must be a visiting home nurse, but this was a guy. Since when did the nursing service let guys in? Hello, what was going on?

I felt my hand being shaken for a fraction too long, then his body brushed past mine. For a brief second the scent of antiseptic and his aftershave wafted over me, as he turned and smiled. Ignoring any misgivings, I smiled back. My heart lurched betrayingly. Shit, Sophie, I told myself, get a grip. Only in books does anything happen between people that quickly.

'Hi, I'm Ben. Sophie, is it? Just getting some more dressings from the car. You can go in, or wait outside if you prefer, I don't mind.'

The sight of Mr Saporiski propped up in bed alarmed me; his wan face peered in my direction, his legs stuck out like icy pole sticks. White skin with angry red welts were weeping tears of clear liquid.

'It's the diabetes, my dear,' he said by way of explanation. 'A nurse comes in twice a week to dress my legs and check my blood sugar. Bloody ulcers, nothing seems to clear them up permanently. They get better, they get worse, then they get better again. Ah, enough complaining, sit down and talk to me. Come closer, I like a pretty face,' he joked 'especially yours.'

As the male nurse's fingers deftly bound the suppurating sores, I looked at his eyes whilst they were focussed elsewhere. OK, brown eyes were good in my books, or any colour for that matter if they were attached to such an eligible male. Then they flicked up at me and returned my gaze. Shit again. As if I was a schoolgirl again, I blushed at being caught out.

All too soon the nurse left.

Reading my work up to where the 'blockage' had happened only took a couple of afternoons. Even so, I couldn't read for long before Pieter's eyelids drooped. Several times it appeared he'd fallen sleep but when I stopped, his eyes opened questioningly.

'So Sophie,' he said with his thick Polish accent, 'tell me about yourself.'

For a long moment I hesitated. What was there to say? My life was pretty pre-ordained, but then again my neighbour was a journalist, maybe he needed some background before he offered advice on my writer's block.

So I told him.

At the end I wondered briefly whether he wasn't more a counsellor than a neighbour.

'So Mr Saporiski, I sense you have lived a full life. I've told you my secrets, but what about yours?'

He shrugged his shoulders, as if no-one would be interested. He was wrong because I was.

'You have family?' I wondered why no one appeared to visit. Not that I was mounting an observation, but the only one who came was the district nurse. That was when my pulse inexplicably rose, I cursed myself, before deciding to drop in next door again. Before the nurse left, of course.

'No, there is no one,' he replied.

Maybe that was why we were attracted to one another. Like minds, no family.

When I heard a faint knock on my door one night, I wondered who it could possibly be at that hour. It was too late for religious conversion, door-to-door selling, alternative electricity schemes, mobile phone network sales. I wondered whether I should answer or let whoever it was go away? I decided to answer.

'Ben! What are you doing here?' He was the least likely person I had expected to see.

'Hello, Sophie. I'm sorry it's so late. Can I come in?' his face was half illuminated by the dim porch light.

Could he come in, was the Pope a Catholic? Just how long was it since a human, let alone a guy, good looking or otherwise, had stepped into my place? Ben, the man of my night-time fantasies, could he come in?

'Sure, social or business?' I blurted, sounding sillier by the minute.

'Maybe we can sit down somewhere first. I'm not sure where to start; it could be a long story.'

In the hazily lit ambience of my lounge, Ben seemed a bit uncomfortable at first and somewhat reluctant to divulge the purpose of his visit. But when I slipped out to the kitchen to make us a drink, talking through the 70's meal hatch, a weird sense of rapport descended.

'It's about Pieter, Mr Saporiski, that is, Sophie.'

'Oh right, how is he? Seemed OK this afternoon,' I said, stirring the coffee. Was he sugar and milk or milk, no sugar, I couldn't recall. I put a little of both in and hoped.

'You two seem close,' he ventured. 'I take it that you know he has no family.'

'Hmm,' I said, non-committedly. When a person told you their life story, I thought it came with some conditions. Like confidentiality. Mine did.

'He has complications, diabetic complications. Poor circulation, eyesight's almost non-existent, heart function is compromised. I guess it's true to say he's getting close to the end. Won't entertain going into a hostel either. I'm concerned.'

'Seems fine to me,' I said cheerfully, not completely cured of writer's block and wondering if I ever was going to be.

'Pieter seems to have taken a shine to you. I was wondering if you could keep an eye on him for me. With his diabetes he could take a sudden turn for the worse and we wouldn't know.'

'Sure,' I said, more convincingly than I felt. If I only had to make a phone call, what could be easier? What Ben didn't know was that I was next to useless in medical matters.

Diabetics had 'hypos' from what I'd heard, but whether you gave them sugar or insulin I hadn't the foggiest. As for injections, I couldn't bear looking at my own arm when the needle went in. All too often it occurred.

Ben left his email address with a series of phone numbers, interestingly including his own mobile. That was enough to make me wonder whether I could possibly read anything else into its inclusion. Also, something I couldn't exclude, deep down he was a sharing, caring person. Wow!

'Maybe we could have a coffee sometime,' I blurted, instantly regretting the impression that I could be seen as a desperate female anxious to bed anything with two legs. Ben had headed for the door so quickly I'd been caught unawares.

For several long seconds he hesitated.

'No, no, I don't think so,' he said. His abrupt departure left a hole in the night.

As I returned to my computer keyboard and turned on the beast, hoping to capture a few more elusive words before midnight, there was another knock at the door.

'What!' my patience was at an end, ' ... Ben?'

'Sophie. I'd love a coffee sometime. Sorry.' This time he really left, leaving me wondering. Still I got half a page down that night before getting too drowsy for coherent thought. Was my block somehow loosening?

Usually on a daily basis I'd drop in on my writing mentor, sometimes bearing some scones, other times a sandwich or two. A sort of easy rapport developed, the one fellow writers have.

'Hi Pieter, how's it going?'

'Ah Sophie, if I was younger ... Now are you going to read to me?' he said, giving me a strange thrill.

'No, not this time. I've got a better idea. Tell me about your life; I've a feeling there could be a story lurking between your words.'

And so I listened to Pieter's story, much more interesting than what I was imagining back home. He told me about his youth, growing up in occupied Poland during the Second World War. The experiences of a teenager growing up dodging bombing and German occupation left me on the edge of my seat. As more and more of his extended family left to seek shelter in safer and further away places, Pieter saw his immediate family dwindle. Then when Soviet occupation occurred in 1944, his life changed yet again. For me, it was an incredible story, and one more deserving of print than my blocked novel. Over several days Pieter recounted his eventual voyage to Australia as a migrant in the early 50's, settling here, marrying and finding work. Probably he never noticed the digital recorder I'd placed by my side.

'No family?' I said, thinking I already knew the answer.

'There was a boy,' he said, looking distantly out towards the window 'from my first marriage, but I lost contact many years before.'

And so that became my story, a story that had to be told.

I couldn't wait to get home and get it all down. That night the keyboard ran hot. Then to find his son, that would be next.

As luck would have it, it was during a moment listening to Pieter that I had a fit. One minute I was chatting in Pieter's lounge, the next I was gone. No warning, nothing. The sky turned black, bright stars shone then faded as I vanished from sight beyond the horizon. My consciousness disappeared as if by the wave of a magic wand.

Coming to, the sensation was all too frequently familiar: a pounding headache; sensitivity to light; urine soaked legs and a strong tendency to tears. Just why was I an epileptic? I had yet to find an answer.

'It's OK, Sophie,' I heard a distant but somewhat familiar voice say. 'You can relax, it's over.'

Gradually my breathing slowed. My surroundings came into focus, an anxious face peering into mine. Just who was he again? That was right, Ben. Ah, shit! Of all the people to see me this way.

'A petit mal, I would say,' he said in a clinical tone, 'what are you on?'

'Epilim,' I mumbled as he nodded.

'How long how have you been epileptic?'

I paused. How did I describe a life in which everything was inseparable, parents, grandparents, siblings, school, friends all inextricably intertwined with fitting? It was as much a part of my life as my right hand. At least the doctor's diagnosis and medication had helped but just as I would never be removed from my right hand, I would never not be epileptic. Just as my right writing hand had shaped my life, so had my fitting defined me for all 29 years of my life. Inexplicable, unpredictable, this was who I was. Epileptic. Couldn't hold a licence, rarely went out, reliant on medication and had to wear an emergency bracelet, who would want me for a friend?

'As long as I can remember,' I said, looking away into the far distance. Not the result of an accident but from an uneventful birth, this was who I was. But like all the others, he'd soon leave. Who'd want to be with an epileptic, waiting in suspense for the next seizure? I don't think so.

'Let's take you home and get you into the shower,' he said pragmatically, ushering me towards the doorway. For a moment I hesitated, he pushed a little harder and I relented. Like a kid caught out wagging school he led me home next door and waited outside my shower. When I emerged in a bathrobe a little later, he gave me a quick reassuring hug and left. Of course, he was a nurse, that's why he cared. Or that's what I told myself.

'Maybe you should think about Trileptal, Sophie, it's a more recent anti-seizure drug. Has the specialist mentioned it?' he said, his brow furrowed in thought as he spoke.

This was all my fault. His little white car was next door, so I had slipped in to say hello. Then I got roped into making us all a drink out in Pieter's kitchen.

'What are you now, a doctor?' I said with a defensive tone in my voice. OK, so he'd seen me at my worst but did that give him the right to make suggestions over my vulnerability? Was he now prying into my life? I was perfectly fine before; his upraised hands rose between us.

But Ben had flinched at my words; his weird reaction getting me thinking. Could there be more to him than he was letting on? Somehow I sensed another story, an intrigue at the very least. It didn't help that I really, really liked him. Alright, I was falling for him.

'What are you two doing out there, I ask you?' thundered a voice from the lounge. 'Where is that drink I hear so much about but see so little of?'

Instantly I stood further away from Ben. Somehow we had inched closer together, probably to keep our voices low for Mr Saporiski's sake. One thing about him, age had not dulled his ancient hearing.

'Tomorrow lunchtime down at the shopping centre, the Bagel shop, 12 on the knocker alright?' Ben whispered, his breath warm in my ear. 'Can't stay long between visits, lunch is half an hour tops.'

I nodded conspiratorially and headed out to my impatient neighbour with his coffee.

'I think you should know, if we're going to be friends, that is,' Ben started, speaking quite tentatively as if he was going to reveal he was married with ten kids or that his father was a mass murderer. 'I actually was a doctor, well, studying to be one anyway.'

'Right,' I gulped before blurting, 'What happened?'

'I developed a liking for pethidine.'

'Oh.'

Ben went on in faulting fashion to tell me how his addiction developed, how it affected him and when he got found out. Somewhere along the way my hand found his, a warm gentle hand at that, which was when his recounting became more fluent. As a hospital intern he'd had relatively easy access to drugs but eventually someone noticed the ever increasing discrepancies between patients and the drug cabinet inventory that defied explanation. Amazingly, the pethidine didn't stop him from working as a doctor, indeed his colleagues were shocked to hear of his habit; they had no idea. It was the CCTV camera that finally exposed Ben, something he showed little bitterness over. But the loss of his job, the shame and the court's demand for drug rehabilitation caused the most hurt. One minute he was treating addicts in Emergency and the next he was sitting alongside them in rehab.

Strangely, he was almost grateful, relieved certainly, for his exposure. The medical board wanted to retain his expertise, he said, so monthly tests were a non-negotiable condition of his parole; the role of nurse a favour wrangled by a family connection. This baring of his soul was as revealing as if he'd stood naked in front of me, this is who I am, he was saying with absolutely no pretence – the lesson to me was salutatory. Hadn't I stood in the shower naked to him too?

'Thanks, Sophie, you're a good listener. Non-judgemental,' he said, 'I've never told anyone about this.'

'Maybe you should have,' I said, all this when I was just as bad at denial. 'No point in denying your past. You've turned your life around, what else could anyone ask?'

'Indeed. What are you doing tonight?' he said catching me unawares. 'Like to catch a movie? Have to warn you though.'

'Of what?'

'I may kiss you in the dark,' he said, a cheeky grin escaping from the side of his mouth.

And he did.

By now I was busy several hours each day at the keyboard with paid work that demanded precedence. But it was Pieter's story that filled in the missing gaps. With the help of Google and a lot of imagination, I had narrowed down my search for his son to two cities, Adelaide and Sydney. Fortunately his was not a common surname but marriage had sullied the waters and no one person fitted the profile exactly. The Privacy Act was fighting the Freedom of Information Act so it was proving more difficult and taking longer than expected. Trying to get the recent crucial Births, Deaths and Marriages information was like trying to extract teeth from a Tasmanian tiger.

My earlier visit next door had proved uneventful. Pieter and I chatted whilst he ate my lamb casserole. Unbeknown to me he had detected my interest in his nurse, something that gave him great pleasure. What is it about people when they try to match others together? Did he see what I couldn't?

'Ah, Sophie, he is a good man. You should listen to your heart.'

'Oh yeah and what is it saying?' I prompted.

'Make the most of your life, not everything is perfect, nor are we. You should not erect walls around yourself, something I did all my life. Yes, build walls, that is what I did.'

Right, so my writing benefactor had transformed into a philosopher and life coach.

But now he was sitting motionless in his lounge chair. My writer's block suddenly paled into insignificance when the ambulance finally arrived. Pieter would be giving no more advice. Now he was beyond reproach and our world. Probably a heart infarction, a heart attack, they said. Not uncommon with his condition or at his age, they said. Nothing could have been done, they said, he died peacefully. That we should go the same way, the older one said. Death can be quite traumatic, we should be grateful on his behalf. Yeah, right. Sorry you died before I finished what I had started.

When Ben turned up the next day, he seemed almost surprised at Pieter's death. Seems like no one can predict our exact passing after all. Not even the medical profession.

'Just when I was trying to discover the rest of his family,' I said. Would he please hold me, I hoped.

'Sophie, I think you should know I found a record of his son amongst the 'Adelaide Advertiser's deaths column. He showed me a computer print out of the death notice showing Pieter's son had died of cancer at age 60.

'Oh.'

'But there is a mention of a grandson, do you see that?' he leaned back against me, his finger pointing out the name. 'Maybe you could send Pieter's story to him.'

I kissed my benefactor. 'Have I told you lately that it's been three months since my last fit? Shouldn't we celebrate?' Fit free, I felt like a new person, one that had a future.

He kissed me back. 'Are you saying I should stay for tea?'

And he did.

'Don't suppose I'll see much of you around here now,' I fished. Was this a crossroads for Ben and me?

'Oh, don't know about that, Sophie. I've just picked up another patient, funnily enough nearby at number 22. So I'll probably be dropping in, if you want to see me, that is,' his casual hint subtle as a bulldozer.

'Number 22? That's next door on the other side. And if I asked you to stay the night, would you?'

'Might,' he said quite nonchalantly, as if he was expecting this. 'What's for breakfast?'

Typical male, I thought, communicates through his stomach. Then Ben let out a chuckle. You'll keep, I thought. With his hand resting on my shoulder, one of his deft fingers had strayed under my twisted bra strap, lingering in the straightening and proving to be the most erotic sensation I'd ever felt. But it was then I knew we had a chance at life together. If he kept that up we'd be arrested for lewd behaviour. Attraction and love is strange, eh?

'Thought you'd be interested though, Sophie.'

I raised my eyebrows.

'Pieter was a lovely old Polish stonemason, but this new guy at number 22's a retired newspaper journalist, could have been helpful for your writer's block, eh?'

Bayerische Motoren Werke

Working in a BMW dealership had its upsides and its downsides. Downsides included: mediocre wages; dirt-engrained hands and the seemingly automatic right for clients to speak down to us. After all I was just a commonplace mechanic.

'I only wish to speak to the Service Manager,' they'd say with condescending accent, 'he'll know what to do.' It was like they were comparing us to the old organ grinder and his trained monkey rattling the tin afterwards. Little did they guess it was grease monkeys in overalls like me that actually fixed their cars leaving others wearing ties to take all the glory, and money.

Upsides? Well, can't recall any at the moment; let me think for a bit. Ah yes.

The Holy Grail for us minions, by the upper echelons of management, was to become 'Employee of the Month.' Staff nominated by satisfied clients got a plastic-coated certificate, handy for a placemat, I thought, and a local restaurant voucher, but who could I take? Cash would have preferable; I was still saving for a deposit so I could apply for a loan to raise the bond on a rental place.

Autoclassics was an ultramodern type of dealership, the white painted workshop area overlooked by walls of glass from where our bosses could watch us and customers could observe their cars being serviced. It all came to a grinding halt when some astute customers began comparing the time charges against their observations. Blinds were soon fitted and we could pick our noses or scratch our bums again in private.

The Managing Director was passionate about Customer Service; possibly one of the reasons I had been sent on the same course several times, somehow centring around my 'attitude.' The MD had been preaching for us to portray a more client focused image; we were all ambassadors for BMW after all, he said. Quite possibly my aside to a workmate, 'Is that why you drive a Lamborghini?' was a whisker too loud. Why was everyone listening in I ask? OK, so I shouldn't have made the comment, I know that now. You could have heard a two hundredth millimetre feeler gauge drop afterwards. My lack of customer skills also extended to the fairer sex which might explain why I wasn't getting any. Also strictly banned were 'liaisons' with clients ever since a salesman had been caught parking his 'car' in the MD's wife's 'garage' while the MD was on the golf course!

This particular day, everyone including the Service desk was flat out except me; a Gold card bearing client's car had broken down, could the dealership respond urgently? I gained the impression it was a matter of life and death.

'Go,' the Service Manager mouthed as he held the phone to his ear. Then he 'zipped' his fingers across his lips. OK, so I had loose lips, ones that got me into messes but not always out of them.

'Go on, take the service vehicle,' he said, throwing keys and impatiently waving me on my way.

The BMW Z4 convertible had stopped on the city side of the Causeway and frankly I was amazed to see it there. This was another of the brand's most reliable models - they rarely gave us any trouble and had one of the lowest warranty costs for the German manufacturer. Dealership protocol also demanded we get the vehicle going or removed from the scene as quickly as possible. There was only negative advertising value from a vehicle broken down alongside a busy highway, no matter what the reason.

'Ah, you've come at last,' said the female private school, mid 20's voice through the driver's side window. 'I was beginning to think the company had deserted me. The Beemer was just serviced the other day and the restaurant only serves breakfast until 11 am.'

'Sorry Ma'am,' I said, putting on my most sympathetic look, 'Superman was called away at the last minute to save the world so they sent me instead.'

A puzzled expression was her reply.

'Can you spell your name?' I asked, looking down at the name A. Forsyth half obscured with masticated chewing gum on the client's identification card.

Yuck! For a moment I wondered whether BMW should have provided a repository for gum instead of the six drink holders, four junk compartments and three ash trays.

'Yes,' she said, glancing at me somewhat challengingly, 'Can you?'

'Could you have run out of fuel, Ma'am?'

'What do take me for, a total idiot?'

'No,' I murmured, 'not total.'

I pulled the bonnet release before she could reply and headed underneath to a safer, more familiar haven, an engine that responded logically to certain stimuli. No weird emotional stuff in the engine bay, definitely a man's world.

A couple of minutes later I determined the problem.

'Well?' she demanded, her eyes flashing.

'It appears to be some sort of an ecological fuel minimalism strategy,' I said.

'Translated?'

'You've run out of petrol.'

Ms Chewing Gum glowered, so much so I could have read the West Australian.

Ten minutes after that, she left with our emergency five litres of petrol transferred to the Z4's tank. Apparently her mobile phone held more interest than the fuel gauge.

Before she left, Ms Chewing Gum insisted that I record a flat tyre instead.

'My father will kill me otherwise,' she said, giving a too-quick smile of expensive orthodontic-straightened teeth.

'We live in hope,' I muttered under my breath. Oh dear, the window was down and she might have heard. Unfortunately, I had failed to step back as Ms Chewing Gum took off like the devil and she drove over my shoe as she headed for her friend's. If not for the obligatory steel-capped boots it would have been a bruised foot and five black toenails. Could I have claimed that on Worker's Compensation, I wondered.

No Employee of the Month's nomination on this call-out.

When, a couple of weeks later, the same car details come up on the iPad computer screen we used, I questioned what anyone could do to deserve this. All because of trying to earn a little more, I had elected to do some night call-out shifts on the BMW 24 hour Roadside Assistance service.

'Brake failure' read the fault message, accompanied by a street location and GPS coordinates. I couldn't wait.

I arrived at the destination. Her Z4, worth about three years of my wages, wouldn't be going anywhere soon judging by the frontal damage, the sturdy Albany Highway gumtree emerging victorious from the 'ergonometric assignation'. Ten grand's worth and at least a month to fix, I quickly estimated. In other words, only a light 'love-tap' for a BMW.

'Ah there you are, at last,' she drunkenly slurred, coming out of the shadows, 'the brakes gave way, I was for-for-for-fortu-fortu, lucky to escape with my life.'

Not only had her tongue developed a life of its own, under the street lights I could see one of her boobs was about to liberate itself from her skimpy dress that was more suited to drying dishes, the front gaping down past her diamond studded bellybutton. Hadn't she heard about double-sided tape? At least the dress should have been cheaper than most due to the lack of buttons, zips and amount of material used, but probably wasn't.

Her boozy breath took mine away. If I'd been breathalysed it would have read over the limit.

'You've been drinking,' I said reprovingly.

'Just a wee bit tipsy,' she giggled, 'not that's any of your business.' Then her eyes tried to focus on me. 'Oh it's you, I should have guessed, the smart arse. Well, don't just stand there, do your magic and get that heap of German scheibe going again.'

'No can do,' I sighed. 'Miracles we do straight away, the impossible takes a little longer, but I will ring for a tray top and a taxi.' I said pushing my mobile phone's pre-dial.

Her eyes continued to squint, 'Are you trying to take the piss?'

'No way, Ma'am, you're doing that quite well by yourself.'

'Where's Adam?' she said, blearily peering into the car. Ah, so that explained the open passenger side door.

'I suspect he's gone to look for another Eve in the Garden of Eden, but there's a lot of fruit left behind,' I said, leaning in and quickly palming the foil packages, condoms and tablets lying scattered on the empty seat.

'Could have been hurt when the air bags didn't go off,' she garbled.

'You were probably going too slow to activate them.'

'Well, smart arse, Adam thought I was going too fast, so there.'

I sighed. Was there no hope for Beemer owners? Did they think they were impervious to life's forces of physics?

'I'm not going home in a taxi, what would my parents say? The brakes failed, I tell you. Anyway, do you know who my father is?'

Keeping a straight face, I replied, 'That's something you should ask your mother. She'd know better than me, pick a private moment though,' the advice flying over her blonde tips at a hundred miles per hour.

Over the next minutes I organised the tow truck, however getting a taxi on a busy Saturday night proved more problematic.

Her manicured fingernail probed my chest. 'You don't like me, do you? I could get you sacked like, like, like …' she said, vainly trying to click her fingers.

Ms Chewing Gum looked down at them as if there were suddenly more fingers than the five she was used to.

'It's my job to fix the car, not your life,' I said. Realising that she didn't live that far from my place; maybe it would be easiest to get Ms Chewing Gum out of my hair, figuratively speaking that is, if I dropped her off home myself. By now the Z4 had been winched onto the truck, it was midnight; officially my callout duties and shift was over.

'Come on, love,' I said, guiding her towards the firm's service vehicle, its brilliant orange hazard lights flashing down the street, warning all but also attracting everyone's attention.

'Don't you 'love' me,' she said, twisting away from me.

Unfortunately this was all that took for her left boob to escape the confines of the 'tea towel' dress. For a split second I nearly offered to help put it back, but that could have been tempting fate a little too much.

'That's entirely your loss, I can assure you, Ma'am.'

Then, from the corner of my eye I saw a white checked Commodore bedecked with red and blue coloured lights rapidly approaching. I guessed they mightn't be so open-minded about the low amount of her breath in the alcohol fumes.

'Quick,' I said, bundling her into the passenger's seat, 'the constabulary's here.'

'Well, don't perve,' she said, 'I'm not wearing any undies.'

As she fell in I shook my head, sprinted around and closed her door by accelerating away quickly. Could it get any worse?

As we drove along I stole an occasional glance at my passenger, who was now rapidly falling asleep. It was obvious an expensive Penrhos education had been wasted, but I had to admit she was quite cool, especially when she kept her mouth closed. Not much younger than my 25 years, under vastly different circumstances I would have liked to have known her better. Maybe if she'd had to work after school like my work mates had she would have appreciated the family's obvious wealth instead of flittering it away on losers, along with her life. Many of our customers were like this; the car was a status symbol to be socially flaunted, the fact that it was a means of transport appeared a bonus. It was so incongruous when I thought of my mum bringing us two kids up by herself without a single word of complaint or bitterness about relying on government handouts after my father had shot through for a 'holiday' in Broome. A holiday that continued 27 years later, I might add.

'We're here now,' I said loudly, but only one of us was awake. She was out of it, eyes firmly closed; her head sagged against my shoulder. Asleep or unconscious, it was hard to say. Even pushing her upright did nothing so, leaving her in the car, I rang the doorbell – no answer. Shit! Raiding her handbag I discovered many things. Apart from the mobile phone, her Gucci handbag was more like a chemist's shop with perfume, more chewing gum, condoms, tablets of all shapes and sizes, multiple lipsticks, her lacy underwear and phew, a set of keys, one of which opened the front door. Hoo-bloody-ray.

I guess I was halfway up the stairs to what could be presumed was her bedroom, the stolen sign said 'Danger-Keep Out,' when a door burst open alongside and an old grey-haired ghost in gaping pyjamas thrust his head out, his mouth like the Polly Farmer tunnel. In the gloom we must have looked quite a sight as I carried Ms Chewing Gum, her tea-towel dress had ridden up, my hands felt only bare flesh, her boob was still hanging out and she had her arms draped around my neck.

Kicking the bedroom door open, I lowered her onto the bed and went to make good my escape.

'What the hell's going on?' the guy I presumed to be her father demanded. If only his pyjamas weren't gaping wide open he could have commanded more respect. But then with that withered equipment maybe he couldn't have fathered her after all.

'Her car came to a sudden stop,' I improvised. 'Your daughter's OK, could be shock, just needs a good night's sleep, be fine in the morning.'

Brushing past him I took the stairs two at a time and pulled the door closed behind me. Far out, what a close call.

Still, no hope of an Employee of the Month nomination again.

'Could the technician who worked Roadside in Vic Park last night come to the office, whoever you are? Staff are reminded personal calls are not permitted during work hours.'

'Phone,' Ms Microphone mouthed, pointing. Didn't she think I knew what one looked like?

'Hello.'

'It's Amelyn; is that the guy who answered my breakdown call last night?' a familiar voice asked. Oh no, I thought, I've got a stalker, but one with an interesting name.

'Yeah, what seems to be the problem?' I said, conscious that all the office staff was

listening in.

'It appears I owe you some thanks and I don't even know your name.'

'No, you don't either,' I said.

She waited for several seconds before continuing, 'Right, but listen, when do you think the car will be ready?'

'Hard to say, Ma'am, maybe four to six weeks, could even be longer,' I said.

'Oh,' she hesitated, 'is there any way it could be done faster, say a week? My father thinks it's in for a simple brake fault.'

This time it was my turn to hesitate. I sighed. 'I'll see what I can do.'

'I owe you big time.'

You sure do, I thought. Just why I was going to so much trouble it was hard to say. Then a sudden idea came to me.

'Tonight, Leisurelife Basketball Centre, six o'clock, it's the end-of-season match and wind-up BBQ afterwards,' I said, before wondering just who I was trying to fool.

Ms Chewing Gum was way out of my league, not that she was likely to come.

'Oh, but I can't tonight, some friends ...' I put down the phone cutting her off midstream. Behind me the Service Manager laughingly made a clenched fist salute and slapped his biceps. Yeah right, as if.

This time it was my jaw that dropped like one of our express car hoists. My mates and I were milling around the entrance in our gear waiting for the team stragglers to arrive when a taxi pulled up and out got my Ms Chewing Gum, Amelyn. Clad in tight fitting jeans and tailored blouse I wasn't the only guy whose heart missed a beat, but it was me she made a beeline for, throwing her arms around my neck only to plant a huge kiss hard on my lips. I don't know who was more surprised, me, my team mates or their girlfriends. Wow!

Then, during the match, she cajoled the girls into a cheer squad that seemingly whooped and hollered the team to within a point of victory. The charade continued after the match when us guys had showered and headed out to the BBQ area. Happily chatting amongst the girls was my 'date'; apparently she knew a couple of them from Vic Park Primary school days.

A charred steak sandwich and glass of wine later, having conquered the female enclave, Amelyn left them and entered our male domain. The guys quickly made a space for her as she oohed and aahed her way through the match highlights, a stubbie now in her hand, each point being embellished as the beers went down south. Strangely, it made little difference that we had lost the match, everyone was excited; it was then I realised her arm was entwined in mine, something that felt kinda nice, I had to admit. A sheer class act or was it? Not only had she hijacked my friends but my emotions too. Amelyn made me want to be half a couple rather than all of a loner. Had I misjudged her?

The evening ended not long after; most of us having to work the next morning, but my estimations amongst my friends had soared to unassailable heights.

'I'll take you home now,' I said.

'No, thanks, Mr Mechanic,' she countered, 'I've called a taxi to go on to a party.'

Cheekily pinching my bum, her final words were, 'We're even now,' leaving me contemplating my navel. Even if she had only been playing along, it didn't explain my confused feelings.

What should I do about it? I wasn't sure.

And when her number came up on my phone that night just as I was falling asleep, what did I do? Nothing. For me to voice my innermost thoughts, radio silence seemed the best policy.

As fate would have it I got lumbered a couple of weeks later with a troubled near-new 650, one that had baffled all the other guys too. To add insult to injury it was Mr Gaping Pyjamas' car, top of the range and worth about five years of wages.

Intermittent faults are a mechanic's worst nightmare, the most difficult to find. Even our most sophisticated electronic diagnostic tool couldn't find the elusive fault – all we knew was that the engine sometimes stopped without warning and, after an hour or two of cooling down, restarted normally. I suspected a faulty ignition pick-up or air flow sensor but every test proved OK. The 650 was the latest model, we had no spares and the boss frowned on swapping parts from another vehicle, especially as the only other one was in the showroom with a deposit on it.

As standard procedure at this point was to plug in the diagnostic tool and drive the vehicle around normally until the fault occurred, then frantically test every component individually, in desperation my boss agreed I could use the car personally for a few days in order to find the problem. The customer had been given a loan vehicle; I was confident we would strike it lucky by then.

Then, as I was stopped at the Oats Street railway crossing and was daydreaming away, the passenger side door was flung open and a familiar set of legs jumped in. She looked great in a white sporty sort of top and fashionably frayed shorts; summer was on its way.

'Get going, Mr Mechanic, the gates are up, you can drop me home,' she commanded. 'Anyway, what are you doing in my father's car?'

'Ah, it's like this; we're trying to find the fault,' I said.

'What with your shopping on the back seat?' she said, rifling through the bags. 'I see, lots of fruit and vegies here, very commendable. Still, my father says you're all a bunch of dickheads who wouldn't know their arse from their elbow? Care to comment?' her haughty tone said it all, her green eyes appraising me like a radar screen.

I gathered then that the car had broken down several times involving everyone important in her father's life. Guessing he was pretty browned off was apparently putting it mildly.

'Well, we are,' I laughed, 'but hey, shit happens. No one's hurt are they?'

I felt Amelyn's eyes continue to study me as we drove, the silence was quite tangible.

'You're different to the guys I usually go out with,' she said with a thoughtful note, 'very different.'

'Lucky them,' I laughed and she joined in.

Amelyn's laugh came from deep down, her eyes smiled at the same time quite delightfully and probably something she didn't do often enough. She was a 'toucher'; it didn't escape my attention that her hand had lightly rested on my leg every time she spoke, as if for emphasis.

'Did you know you make me laugh?' she said, her eyes shining like emeralds.

'No, but just hum the tune and I'll join in,' I said, smiling.

It seemed my attempts at humour were paying dividends as she laughed again. Very infectious.

All too soon we pulled into her driveway but I didn't have to turn the engine off, the 650 had stopped of its own accord and we rolled the last few metres, the only sound the crunching of gravel under the wheels. Reaching down to the diagnostic tool I quickly checked for fault codes. None. But with no time to waste, I pulled the bonnet release, ran around, leaned underneath and removed the engine covers.

Wanting to back probe the air flow sensor, I yelled out to Amelyn, 'Quick, can you pass me the multimeter on the floor? Looks like a phone.' Reaching back without looking, my hand encountered something deliciously soft that definitely wasn't her hand. With a laugh she prised my fingers from her breast and put the meter into my hand.

'Sorry,' I muttered, my blush hidden by the latent waves of heat washing over me under the bonnet. As I probed, the display flickered, ah yes, there it was, the little bastard. Gotcha, I thought, open circuit and the sensor was overly hot, just like my face.

'Amie dear, what's going on?' came another known voice, but one that had little welcome.

Oh shit, not him, not now!

Without thinking I straightened up in shock, the sharp bonnet hook neatly gouging my scalp, then when I glanced over to Amelyn she had my large black hand print on her top, right over her breast. Mr Gaping Pyjamas followed my line of sight and began to turn a colour known as Crimson Red on the BMW paint chart. As blood trickled down my face he looked like an apoplectic fit wasn't far away. Still, it's amazing what surgical options are available these days and, unlike me, he probably had top medical cover.

'I'd pack your tools when you get back, young man. It's obvious you prey on the young and vulnerable female customers,' he spoke with enough venom to put a dugite to shame.

'But Dad ...'

'No Amie, he's been leading you astray, drinking at all hours. It's got to stop, you understand? Your mother and I didn't raise you for this sort of life. First of all those revolting piercings, next you'll have McDonalds tattooed on your bum.' Then turning to me, 'Leave the car, it's also obvious you haven't got the faintest clue what's wrong or how to fix it. I'll get it towed back at your firm's expense. Try catching a bus, they're more reliable than that Kraut crap heap,' Mr Gaping Pyjamas grumbled. He went inside, presumably to seal my fate via the phone.

As I gathered up the diagnostic equipment in abject resignation, the front door opened. Amelyn had returned with a damp washer and began to bathe my forehead.

'Quite the hero, even spilling blood for me,' she said with a disarming smile.

Immediately the gouge stopped hurting. Up close Amelyn was even more disconcerting, how could I be mad at her?

'I'm sorry,' she said, words I never expected to hear.

Our eyes locked, then hands pulled my head down to her level. 'For compensation,' she whispered as her lips enveloped mine.

Returning Amelyn's kiss, I suddenly felt inspired. What did I have to lose? Nor did she mind my tongue. No way was I going to be the first to stop either. Instinct took over. After several minutes of my most inspired pashing she was the first to come up for air. Then just to be sure, we did it again.

'Wow,' she said, finally surrendering, 'that made me squirm.'

I hoisted the gear under my arm. 'Got to go, see ya around.'

'And Mr Mechanic?'

'Yeah?'

'It's not over,' she said with a mysterious look. 'Trust me.'

Arriving back at work an hour later all sweaty and smelly from lugging the gear a kilometre from the bus stop, my destination was the Service Manager's office.

'No point beating around the bush, Brett mate, the shit's hit the fan on this one,' he said, leaning forward.

Andrew was our team's Goal Attack; many had been the time I'd flick-passed the ball to him under pressure when he'd scored in spectacular fashion.

'Right,' I said, 'do I get a chance to explain?'

'Nah, don't bother, I've got to let you go. Sorry, Brett, but that's just the way it is, especially fraternising with customers,' he spoke quite loudly so Ms Microphone could hear.

With me beginning to see everyone in a new light lately, he continued in a whisper, 'Come back to see me on the quiet when all this little lot blows over. The man's a prick but a good customer and influential over there,' he flicked his eyes over to the offices where the MD sometimes resided when he could be bothered. 'Wesley school tie and all that,' he said, putting on a plummy accent.

Picking up my tools, I said my farewells to the guys in the workshop but left via the spare parts counter. I leant right over to attract my best Defence player's attention.

'Hey Philippe, can you order in an air flow sensor for a petrol Series 6, 650 from Germany? But no one is to know,' I tapped the side of my nose. 'Premiers next year, eh?'

'Si, pronto amigo, maybe cuatro, cinco days, OK? Uno week max. Premiers, yeh.'

Back at work the following Monday, Mr Gaping Pyjama's 650 was sitting forlornly in the corner, its silver bonnet raised as if in surrender. My workmates all gathered around clapping me on the back and saying how well the place had run without me. Liars all of them, but commonplace people and great mates.

'Team practice starts next month,' I said with a wry grin. 'No booze, no drugs, no sex, alright?'

After much booing, 'Service Manager wants to see you,' they said, breaking into an 'oohing' session. Right.

'You wanted to see me?'

'Yeah, listen mate, that bloody 650's still here and I thought we won the war too. Everyone's had a go, any ideas? Even Munich's stuffed, never heard of the problem. Trouble is the owner's throwing a real wobbly, threatening a law suit based on the 'Lemon laws', you know, and wants a brand new one. But the firm can't afford to budge, not on a two hundred and fifty thousand dollar BMW for Chrissake. Media would go ape-shit too if they got this one on TV.'

'What's in it for me?' I asked.

'Well, Brett, you get your job back for one and into the owner's good books for another. By the way, I want to play another position next season, did I tell you? Maybe Goal Defence, could be easier on my old knees, the wife's complaining, what do you say?'

That morning I installed the new air flow sensor on the 650 and took a closer look at the old one. Very strange. One of the terminals looked like it had been partially severed and was just hanging on by a strand or two. But as to whether it was a production or assembly fault it was impossible to say. From a technical point, the partial break wouldn't have caused a fault code, gone into a base setting or 'limp home' mode either. Was it warranty or not, I wondered.

It was then I was startled out of my reverie as the workshop speaker bellowed, with much finger thumping and heavy breathing beforehand.

'Hey Mr Mechanic, I know you're out there, somewhere,' Amelyn's voice came over loud and clear. 'Listen, I don't know how you feel about me, like, I don't even how I feel about you myself, but there is electricity between us, isn't there? Is this microphone working?' she said in a loud aside.

All around me there was an automatic murmur of assent. I cringed. What a crazy kid, high maintenance, but maybe she was right. Could it be we did have something? A certain something to last more than a week, a month, a year, a lifetime, who could say?

'And,' she continued, 'would you believe I got a job the other day, like, nothing fancy but it's a start. Hey, I know you're an OK guy, I thought you would have found it by now, but my nail file was blunt. What do you reckon? Are we an item or not?'

I sighed.

An enormous roar of passion from the guys surrounded me, I found myself hoisted on their shoulders and carried precariously to be dumped in front of Amelyn.

'You bugger,' I said, shaking my head, then kissing her like my life depended on it 'cause it did.

The Auction

'Lot 52A, a last minute inclusion in your catalogue, Ladies and Gentlemen,' my patter deeply engrained by habit and fatigue, continued in the boring monotone it was.

Never fazed by a last minute inclusion in the day's sales, I automatically read the card thrust into my hands, my mind not registering the words, my tongue never missing a beat. And if I was Maurice Scrimshaws Auction House's best auctioneer why was I paid such a pittance? Wasn't my father the biggest tight wad? His testosterone level was so high hair grew out of nearly every orifice: ears; nose; once I caught him picking a hair from his tongue. Working for family was always a big drawback of my job. Still, once considered a small cog in a big machine, at least I had grand plans. One day the drab viewing and auction rooms would be enlarged and renovated to equal my mother's new granite kitchen. Maybe then we could eradicate the all pervasive musty smell that came with deceased estates. The waft of mothballs and mould hardly created an atmosphere conducive to profitable, frenetic bidding.

'Lot 52A, *a not to be forgotten Mystery Evening with an insatiable lover,*' I nasally drawled. '$50 bids. Do I hear $50?' I said glancing down at the reserve sum on the card.

It was only when I heard a titter break out across the audience like crinkling cellophane, that I guessed something wasn't quite right. By then I was committed, my mind raced ahead. What business was it of mine what Father wanted auctioned? Sons should do as they were told, he said. Sell this, sell that. So I did, no questions asked.

The auction commenced. Like an athlete on adrenalin, the gavel handle in my hand acting as a baton pointer, this was a relay race to the finishing line, but one that I conducted. This was my forté; didn't I have a reputation of selling anything for the most? Once underway, I was an unstoppable automaton, my pride in auctioning unassailable.

'On my left, $50.'

'Gentleman in the centre, $100.'

'At the back, $150.'

'On my left, $200.'

'At the back, $250.'

'Gentleman in the centre, $300.'

'On my left, $350.'

'At the back, $400.'

'On my left, $450.'

After this frantic start, the bidding slowed so I played my trademark trick, tossing the gavel in the air only to catch it by the head. So far I'd never missed the catch. Then, from the corner of my eye, there was a movement. Holding a phone up was Sammy, our secretary, gesturing. She must have left her desk to man one of the room's phone lines and had a bidder on the line. Ah yes, Samantha. With a cleavage that extended down all the way to her 'Navel base' in Antarctica, she was always good to distract many a bidder, not me though. Why would I go out for a hamburger when I could have steak at home, as I'd heard once famously stated? My Naomi was pure prime fillet.

'On the phone, $500,' I said and everyone pivoted to Sammy. It was as though they sensed this lot was unique, especially if it had attracted an outside bidder.

Then, after the shortest of pauses, off we went again.

'On my left, $550.'

'At the back, $600.'

'Gentleman in the centre, $650.'

'At the back, $700.' From the front, I saw the guy in the centre shake his head. OK, so now he was out, but there were still two strong bidders.

'On my left, $750.'

'At the back, $800.'

'On my left, $850.'

'At the back, $900.' But now the speed of the bids was again slowing and, from experience, I sensed the end was getting near. The 'at the back' bidder was fidgeting as if his conscience was pricking at spending so much money on an unknown quantity. Oh well, it was nearly lunchtime and my sandwiches beckoned. What had my live-in girlfriend, Naomi, put in them? Maybe my favourite salami and salad, I could but hope. From my bewildering minx, yesterday's cryptic note tucked in the lunchbox had read, 'I love you but.' What would today's say? This was when something made me glance down at the lot card. The familiar number suddenly stood out as in flashing neon lights.

Shit, what was going on? Why hadn't I noticed this before? How blind was I? More importantly, wasn't that my girlfriend's phone number on the seller's details? Naomi? Was I auctioning my own lover off to the highest bidder? No rationale could explain this. All reason departed. My Naomi? Naomi?

'On my left, $950.'

My 'at the back' bidder shook his head; he was out. The bid was with the guy 'on my left'.

At this I saw an opportunity, my resolve strengthened, my back bone stiffened as I remembered my training in auction rules and protocol.

'We have a house bid, Ladies and Gentlemen. I'm bidding for myself. $1000.' As in Luna Park, a sea of open clown-like mouths in the audience swung towards me.

For 30 seconds my heart bolted up to my mouth. Then plummeted.

'On my left, $1050.'

Sammy raised her hand. 'On the phone, $1100.'

'On my left, $1150.'

'On the phone, $1200.'

I shook my head, what lunacy was this? How could I concentrate when all life around me threatened to dissolve? If auctioning a woman transformed me into a pimp, would the highest bid turn me into a 'punter' as well? Had Naomi become a high class hooker without me knowing? How long had this been going on? How could I end this farce? Would she stop hooking if I proposed? Naomi?

'House bid, $1250.'

'On the phone, $1300.'

'On my left, $1350.'

'On the phone, $1400.' Hmm, I detected more conversation than just another bid. Could the bidder be slowing?

I groaned. Possibly it was triggered by the possibility of losing Naomi, I couldn't be sure. Of course, the thought of some other man sleeping with her stuck like a fish bone in my throat. Why hadn't I married her, maybe that would have stopped her from straying? On the other hand, had I only stumbled on her strange predilections in time to stop me making a complete fool of myself?

'On my left, $1450.'

I let the bid stay there for a full minute. You could have heard a single auction programme rustle, the audience was so hushed. Could it be they sensed some new mating ritual being carried out in front of them, I didn't know? A type of arranged marriage with built-in dowry, I wondered. Was it a voyeuristic view of procurement, where a man bought a woman sight unseen? Only I knew the item being auctioned. Only I knew what she was worth. A rare treasure and priceless. Naomi?

I took a deep breath and was about to bid, only to be beaten.

'On the phone, $1500.'

As an insight came to me, my fuse burst. I'd had enough of this, it was obviously my girlfriend's crazy ploy. Stepping down from the podium, I wrested the phone from Sammy. 'Naomi, is that you? Haven't I told you not to ring me at work? This has gone on long enough. Next time you want shopping money, just ask, alright?' Just possibly my voice was slightly raised. OK, so I shouted.

To this day I suspect Sammy of betrayal. She, of course pleaded the Fifth Amendment. Either way, the 'Speakerphone' button had been pushed down, giving the entire hushed auction room an earful.

Without giving her the satisfaction of a reply I hung up.

I cleared my throat. Several times. At least this gave my face a chance to pale from the blushing. Out front my audience waited with bated breath for the saga's next exciting instalment.

'On my left, $1550.'

'House bid, $1600.'

I glared down from the podium at my competitor. A casual

looking guy, he seemed to be having trouble making up his mind and was searching the ceiling as if for inspiration. A smiling kind of smirk lit his thin face.

Sensing victory was in the offing, I tossed my gavel in the air, this time catching it by the handle. Now I was poised to deliver the coup de grace, somewhat poorer though.

'Going once.'

'On my left, $1650.'

Did my look of dejection show?

'House bid, $1700.'

By now all my auction experience and training had flown out the window, leaving a primeval urge in its place. It was obvious 'on my left' and I were engaged in a duel, the winner taking home the fair maiden as prize. In a previous time we could have been two knights on steeds jousting to win the hand of a beautiful woman, the lance my gavel. Admittedly, my Naomi was especially attractive and my male pride was at risk. Where else would I find someone who set my pulse racing like a Formula 1 race car?

'On my left, $1750.' All this time the hushed audience were poised as if at a grand final tennis match, their eyes rushing from one player to the other and back again with each bid.

'House bid, $1800.'

'On my left, $1850.' The time he took to bid gave me a chance to think about practicalities. From memory my credit card was currently a little burdened with debt, but with luck and some imaginative accounting I could possibly go higher. But not much, the end was in sight one way or the other. Still, the thought of going home at night and not being greeted by Naomi would be the bitterest pill to swallow. Why had I allowed myself to fall in love with her anyway? Was it because I had no choice in the matter? Logic had flown out the window, my heart raced when she kissed me.

'House bid, $1900.'

Possibly I swaggered a bit. But my opposition was now on the ropes, I could feel it. He was wavering ever so slightly. Like Rocky 9, I kept him at arm's length for the last blow, mine, I hoped.

'On my left, $1950.'

I cursed, would this guy ever give up? Maybe I really had met my match. How much was in my wallet? I wondered, searching. Hmm, enough to get home tonight on the bus at least. OK, last bid.

'House bid, $2000.' Quite possibly my voice had taken on a dejected tone. I was done.

Time ticked by, before I came to my senses. 'On my left' hadn't bid. Dare I hope? I raised the gavel.

'Going once.'

'Going twice.'

'Sold. Lot 52A. $2000 to the House.' As the gavel hit its base my relief was palpable.

'Next lot, Ladies and Gentlemen, is Lot 53. Here we have a Blackwood dresser of 1930's vintage.'

Dragging myself up the front steps that night left me unusually exhausted. Now I was broke, but home. On the bright side, it was Friday night and a weekend of blissful sleep-ins beckoned.

'I've had a terrible day, Naomi. Still, here's your money.' I said, passing over the envelope as we kissed, a little perfunctorily on my behalf.

'What money?' Her face took on a puzzled look.

'The auction, what else? You, for the night, you know. Lot 52A, a *'not to be forgotten Mystery Evening with an insatiable lover,'* I repeated.

'I don't know what you're talking about. Do you normally bid for hookers? That wasn't me.'

'It wasn't?' I gulped.

'No, but what did I get? What did you pay?'

'Two thousand bloody dollars, if you must know. Cleaned me right out.'

Her arms snuck around me. 'You're not mad, are you? See it as a test of faith. Of course you seem to have forgotten one thing.'

I raised my eyebrows.

'My joker brother and his new bride were arriving today from London and staying the weekend. By the sounds of it, you've already met him. And, oh yeah, I lent her my phone. Still, now I know my worth, maybe marriage may be cheaper.'

Sex and Drugs
without Music

'… should payment not be received within five working days, the bank will initiate Notice of Foreclosure and eviction proceedings,' stated that night's windowed envelope greeting in the letterbox. Added to the unpaid council and water rates, plus a maxed out credit card, I was in deep excreta. Not only would I be without a roof over my head, my first real job after college was at a critical probationary stage. Paying peanuts too.

Our troubles began when Dad died. With his heart attack occurring in the client's wife's arms whilst lying naked in their bed, it could hardly be said he was measuring up the site for renovations! Sad though it was, my mother's own heart barely missed a beat before she eloped with an American Ambassador's aide who had a commercial TV accent.

'See ya boys,' she yelled, throwing the house keys to us startled sons, 'keep an eye on the house and come visit sometime.'

With a quick wave from our maternal, the black consulate limo took off, its stars and stripes flag fluttering from the radio aerial. Even at age 23 and 25 the shock was complete; we were now on our own for the first time in our lives. Reality hit.

A year later, my younger brother appropriated the last remaining funds from his inheritance, heading overseas to further his education. Contiki 101 he called it, European booze and carouse. His abrupt departure, combined with the bank's demanding letter, left me to flounder before I hit on the real potential of the house. Yes! Requiring only a little imagination and no major structural changes, I wondered if it might make a perfect type of boarding house. Maybe I could rent out the remaining four bedrooms, stave off the bank and keep the house. And that's what I did; survival is a strong motivator.

So it was my father's architectural masterpiece that allowed me to survive. A fan of the Californian bungalow design, he had modelled himself on Frank Lloyd Wright, the famous American architect. Like a starfish, our five bedroom house sprawled itself across a monstrous suburban block. The master bedroom had its own bathroom while each of the other bedrooms was semi-ensuite, lending itself to a kind of semi-independent living for my brother and me whilst growing up. It also meant at night he occasionally snuck in a female 'friend' and my parents were none the wiser.

After a few unpaid rent hiccups from 'boarders', my boss suggested I commission a real estate agent to collect the rent and take on the fictitious role of lease holder and co-boarder. That way I could get the inside info on the other boarders before they flitted leaving a mess, damage or bills behind. It worked, more or less. Apart from the usual hassles of some phantom using all the hot water, and the last square of toilet paper, we all lived in a communal atmosphere not unlike Big Brother. With various boarders coming and going, sometimes I wondered if the house wasn't more of an urban train station. But as long as they paid, how could I complain? In fact, the boarders provided me with a lot of interest; I had no need for friends with the convivial boarders who used my house, or should I say, the boarding house.

Gradually all the rooms got rented, the bills got paid, I almost began to relax.

Until Alison came along.

With mesmerising eyes that followed me around like a CCTV camera, this diminutive part-time uni student failed to fit any stereotypical mould. My boss's crude advice that 'eagles always poo outside the nest' was ever present.

Meantime an errant lock of brown hair barely disguised her ever observant gaze. Intriguing.

'Ooh, ooh, ooh, ah. Ooh, ooh, ah yes, do it to me baby,' were examples of the sounds of someone experiencing exquisite pleasure I heard coming from her bedroom. Even though it was shielded by thick brick walls, no one could miss the unmistakeable sounds of a couple sexually engaged. This was not the first time either. In fact most nights, seemingly sometimes for hours, the noises of human copulation persisted, always different as though she was trying different techniques on different partners. Was Alison a part-time hooker or was it someone else in the house? Arousing at first, but then her appetite for indiscriminate sex began to irritate, especially when I was getting little. Alright, I was getting none! Between my erratic work hours and the right person having yet to appear, my personal life was as barren as the gravel driveway. No matter how many times I told myself to be tolerant, Alison would appear in my dreams to haunt me. Once the orgasmic shrieking grew so loud I thumped on the wall painfully hard. At least my bruised hand was rewarded by a sudden reduction in coital noise; I grinned at the thought of the guy having his jollies cut short. Was she knocking off my cereal as well?

Those hot airless summer evenings, lying on my bed tossing and turning, with all the groaning and moaning, I'd be praying for her to get to where she wanted to be. How long could it take for a woman to get it off? Based on guys, surely a couple of minutes were all that was necessary for nirvana, wasn't it? 'Mona' became her house name, not that anyone was game enough to say it to her face.

Later on I was mostly doing night-shift work so my need for sleep during the daytime rarely coincided with her night-time assignations. Fortunately. How she had the inclination or stamina for such long noisy encounters at the end of the day was beyond my comprehension. Absolutely. I also despaired when all my food seemed to run out at vital times. Short of locking the cupboard, whilst I suspected Alison of misappropriating my favourite, all-natural, hand-mixed muesli, no way could I catch her out. This muesli was my one extravagance, the local Italian store making it to my own secret recipe. Even when I surreptitiously pencilled in level marks on the containers, another lower mark was there the next day. Couldn't even be sure it was Alison; although her vaguely innocent look the few times we sat down to eat together made me suspicious. It was as though she was challenging me. With the kitchen being the focal hub of the house, it was possible others were guilty, but their eyes didn't penetrate me like hers.

What a promiscuous temptress Alison was.

This particular night we knocked off work early, the rain and searching wind driving everyone off the streets. No action.

Slipping off my grubby 'work' clothes, I turned for the bedroom door. It was then I noticed a strip of light from underneath the door. My first thought was that I'd left the light on, something not hard to do during the daytime. Was that a splash?

But little could have prepared me for the centrefold sight. Alison, my boarder. With no sea of foam to obscure vision, indisputably I had a naked female body immersed in my bath. I don't know who was more surprised, her or me. Both looked at one another in shock. Alison?

'What are you doing here?' we spoke as one.

'This is my bathroom,' I said, as she ineffectually tried to hide herself. All I had to do was grab a towel and wrap it around my waist, but it was obvious she felt exposed, and was. Delightfully so. Whether it was to embarrass her or feast on the curves, wet curls and shadows, I can't say. What a view and memory to behold forever. Phew! Alison had the most pert nipples, until she followed my line of vision and tried to cover them. Should I tell her that her other breast was now the most appealing? No! How fortunate were we males that nature had made it impossible for females to cover themselves without the aid of many leaves. All I needed was one long leaf. Well, not so long, although ...

'I thought you were out,' she retorted.

'Obviously not. This is my bathroom,' I repeated emphasizing the 'my', 'you're the one who's trespassing.'

By this time she must have realised I was no pushover. Was she the one raiding my food stash, I still wondered. Alison bore a more guilty look, but not a stitch else. What a sight!

We had the ultimate Mexican stand-off. Trouble was I felt something other than my resolve harden as my towel started to take on a life of its own.

'A gentleman would at least pass me my towel.'

'Never said I was a gentleman,' I smiled, savouring her embarrassment. It almost made up for all those sleepless nights listening to her noisy romantic interludes. Almost, that is.

The stand-off continued. Then Alison did what she should have done earlier, got out of the bath. As 'Aphrodite' rose and stepped over the edge, all would have gone well, but the glossy tiles had always proved slippery for me as well. Falling into my arms, we both went down like skittles, my body bearing the brunt. Ouch!

Pushing herself up off me as decorously as possible, she grabbed her towel and undies from the chair and puddled off. If ever there was an endearing sight, it was the aloofness in which she got up, dripping all over me.

What a woman!

Strength under adversity, what more could you dream of? A laugh escaped before I could stifle it, she turned, poked her tongue out, then smiled. What spirit! It was in that instant that Alison appealed like no one else. Wow!

My last endearing sight was her haughty arse limping through the doorway, the sweetest set of cheeks known to mankind dripping across my Berber bedroom carpet, the faintest aroma of my bath salts lingering.

Niggling at the back of my mind, I wondered if I wasn't to pay a price for that visual tryst.

Hi Sis,

Had an absolute crap day yesterday. Between
an early lecture at uni and my job at the clinic,
Fridays are always a hectic end to the week.
Then when the clinic's hard drive crashed, taking
a lot of my work with it, I got close to tears
until the thought of a long hot bath occurred.
'Mystery man' worked nights – how would he
ever know?

As I eased myself over the bath's edge, the
soothing warmth of the hot water enveloped
me. Oh bliss. Lying back, my body relaxed,
any anxious thoughts soon disappeared into the
steam.

The door bursting open awoke me. Why hadn't
they knocked, I thought, until I realised that
this was someone else's bathroom, not the shower
I usually shared with backpackers. Trying to
shrink down into the water, I wished I could
have been instantly transported back to my room,
preferably fully clothed. The sight of a naked
man overlooking didn't help, especially with all
his dangly bits dangling close by. Good bod, well
equipped, from a strictly professional point of
view, of course. Jamie?

'What are you doing here?' we chorused.

'Thought you were out,' I said, adding, 'I felt
like a bath.' So between the leer and salacious
look on his face, I felt myself blushing. OK, the
sight of nakedness I'm more or less accustomed

to through work but this time something else was going on.

'If you were a gentleman.' I grimaced, 'you would at least pass me my towel.'

'Never said I was a gentleman.' he smiled sweetly, making no attempt to comply. Right, so he was going to make me grovel. Thinking through my options, I suddenly felt empowered and rose from the bath. No way was I ashamed of my body and this self righteous voyeur did not intimidate me. Well, not entirely.

All would have gone well but my foot slipped on the wet tiles; I fell over. Somehow he ended up under me. At least his body proved some use at last, cushioning my fall. Serve him right. Hardly hesitating I stood up and hoped my dripping footprints caused some damage to his carpet. OK, so they wouldn't, no harm in thinking it though is there? Life lacks justice sometimes.

To me it seemed so unfair that he should have the bath. Guys shower but we girls need a bath, don't you agree? OK, so the lease is in his name, but does he have to strut around like he owns the place? It was obvious by the stuff in his bedroom he has expensive taste, although I never see him wear anything else but street grunge. Jamie doesn't fit a mould I know, he keeps himself to himself but I guess working nightshift does that. Pity. What he actually does, no one knows –

'Mystery man' was the nickname I gave him. Of course, the benefits of someone on a reliable wage are widespread; I can always count on snaffling some of his extensive food stash. Not hard to subvert his amateurish detective efforts either; water in the milk, pad the packet bottom, a lower mark on the container, how I love a challenge. Once I even put a plastic toy in his special muesli. Such fun trying to take the smirk off his face.

Talk soon,

Alison

Another boarder was Werner, a backpacking butcher from Germany who thought he was God's gift to women. If you said he had the morals of an alley cat, that was to denigrate the feline species. A different female at the breakfast table each morning, he seemed to think it was his sole role to impregnate every woman that crossed his path and a few that hadn't. Trouble was, unlike me, he had the most powerful weapon known to man, charisma. Once he latched on, he never let go. The girl's fate was set. With Alison just a bedroom away and knowing her predisposition for noisy encounters, I despaired. It was only a matter of time before those two hooked up.

Whack! The sound of hand hitting flesh was unmistakeable. Her bedroom door flew open and Werner tumbled out holding his hand to his cheek. Under his fingers a large red imprint showed. He'd had his first refusal. The look of puzzlement in his eyes was to be remembered. If I was curious about Alison before, I was fascinated now. For such a nymphomaniac to be so fussy …

Hey Sis,

You won't believe what's happened. Right under everyone's noses Jamie was running a clandestine night-time drug factory down the back shed. I've had to move out, the agent can go hang for the last month's rent too. I'll let you know when I find another place. The police took a statement which is attached, but don't think I'll have to give evidence. Phew!

Frantically packing, will ring later.

Alison

Police statement:

On the evening of Friday the 19th August at approximately eight pm, I observed my co-boarder Jamie Milson enter the garden shed in the company of a Caucasian male whom I have identified from photos as Number 14. Approximately 1.8 metres in height, he had tattoos on both forearms, pierced ears and was heavily built. About 15 minutes later they left carrying shopping bags. I rang the drug squad immediately.

I rented a room in the house at 94 Langford

Way, Ferndale for about eight months.
During this time I noticed strong chemical-
like smells coming from the backyard shed
several times as well as guys walking up and
down the driveway at night.

Signed

Alison Wells,

formerly of 94 Langford Way, Ferndale.

The next time I saw Alison, it was six months later. I was
working and her baby was cooing as she rocked the pram.
Sitting between two other very obviously pregnant women
outside the restaurant, Alison's emotive face stood out like
a lit beacon. For a tiny moment our gazes crossed, but she
appeared otherwise preoccupied with her baby. A nose I
would like to have tweaked seemed to twitch back at me as
I passed by on the footpath. Whether she recognised me, I
hoped not, her eyes appeared expressionless. The thought of
her having a child came as no surprise, with all her almost
nightly copulations in the house, she could have populated
Australia single handedly. But of all her chosen bed buddies,
I was not one. I kept walking.

Dear Sis,

*Despite his scruffy clothes, the instant he
walked past, I knew who he was. Bloody Jamie.*

What a cheek! Out of jail already, is there no justice is this crazy world? Seeing I was prime witness to his illegal activities, shouldn't the police have told me he was back on the streets? That's the trouble these days; a proven drug dealer only gets a slap on the wrist with a wet lettuce leaf, as our dear old dad would have said. The weakness of people and the prevalence of drugs can only lead to one thing in my mind – moral decadence.

Which reminds me, I may not have told you of one of my sad exploits ages ago when I was back at the house? You know my acute sensitivity to alcohol, well, one spiked mixed drink and I went under the table at a clinic work function, literally. Apparently they poured me into the taxi, the next thing I woke up in bed in just my bra and knickers. What a revelation that was! As far as I could tell nothing had happened but it was an anxious month or so, believe me. Lemon, lime and bitters is now my poison of choice, no exceptions, I'm never drinking alcohol again. Tell everyone.

Back to 'Mystery man.' It was the flash of little white plastic bags flicking between hands that alerted me, that and the surreptitious exchange of folded banknotes. Shit, Sis, I was witnessing drug transactions under my very nose, again! Did this guy know no limits? Only a few months after being arrested in a drug bust and here he was still dealing. I saw red.

Picking up my mobile and, after a million reconnections, eventually the drug squad answered.

'I know who this prick dealing is. His name is Jamie Milson, 94 Langford Way, Ferndale.'

'Just wait there, don't alert the suspect. We're on our way,' they said.

Just 15 minutes later, a chequered police car pulled up. They bundled Jamie in and took him away at the speed of light. Through the window the look of exasperation on his face was worth it, Sis. Maybe this time they'll put him away for good. Drug dealer scum like him don't deserve compassion, do they?

Inside I felt good. One less dealer on the streets and another blow to someone who'd ruffled my feathers. Do you think I should visit him in jail? No, probably not, but there was something between us that defied explanation in his bathroom that time. Hopefully he has seen the error of his ways.

How is my Arnold there?

Love,

Alison.

Dear Sis,

I was wondering if Garon mightn't become more than a friend. There is definitely something alluring about the sight of a man in uniform, yeah?

When he asked me to accompany him to his graduation, how could I say no? His family would be there, he said, and I tried not to read too much into the occasion. Isn't 25 way too early to settle down, although my thesis is nearly finished according to my uni supervisor. Maybe travel could be my life's next adventure.

What a lot of fuss they make, I thought. The police band discordant as all the uniformed guys strutted around like peacocks. It didn't help that the sun in the stadium seats had nearly put me to sleep.

But listen to this, Sis, sitting up on the stage to receive some commendation or other, was, would you believe it, Jamie the drug dealer and my old co-boarder. I nearly died. Remember, he's the one I dobbed into the police? Twice! Turns out all that time he was an undercover cop. According to the program, the Commissioner's award was for 'outstanding service to the community whilst taking initiative and exhibiting bravery.' A squadron of flies could have flown around in my mouth and landed, I was so jaw struck. 'The award is for reducing the level of drugs in the community using an innovative, hands-on street-level approach. Despite great risk to himself and the need to overcome many obstacles, Detective Milson thwarted drug dealers at their own game, making a real difference. Congratulations.' Can you believe it?

If I could have squeezed between the stadium's boards and slunk home I would have, trust me. Obstacle was now my middle name. My first instincts about him were right after all.

I was edging my date towards the exit when, as luck would have it, Jamie infiltrated himself in front. Aaron automatically extended his hand and offered his congratulations. Of all things, Jamie is now one of the Force's latest high-profile figures to encourage recruitment. A modern day hero, no less. Far out!

'Ah, Alison, we meet again,' he smirked.

Beam me up Scotty, I communicated to the starship Enterprise hopefully hovering overhead.

'You know Alison?' Aaron said, surprise in his voice.

Scotty? Now!

'Used to live together. Very closely. Shared a house,' he smiled sweetly. 'I hardly recognised you with your clothes on.' Aaron gave me a very concerned look. So I deserved it but this was neither the time nor place, was it?

'You could have said,' I started.

Scotty? No, not later, right now!

'Even used the same bath water.'

I poked my tongue out.

'Then there's your baby,' Jamie continued.

By now Aaron was firmly in abandonment mode and desperately trying to sight his parents.

'H-h-he's not really mine anymore,' I spluttered, 'alright, I conceived him but …'

'And what about stealing my cereal? It was like I was feeding the masses.

'Ah, there's Mum and Dad,' my date said, slipping away and leaving me to my fate, 'don't worry, I'll grab a lift with them.'

'It was left out in plain view, what did you expect?' I retorted. 'So I liked the organic oats, sundried sultanas and apricots, anyway you could afford it. We were just poor uni students. You, at least, had a full-time job.'

'Seems to me you could afford to drink.'

My patience snapped, 'I don't drink!'

'Oh, and who was that I found sprawled in her vomit on the front lawn? Made the garden look quite untidy,' he sneered.

'It was just once,' I said, now discovering who'd cleaned me up. And who'd held me over the toilet. And who'd taken my clothes off and put me to bed. Holy shit!

Anyway, any further argument was suspended when some dignitaries came up and led Jamie away for a vote-gaining photo opportunity. Suddenly I felt quite alone.

And now for the past couple of weeks I've been so confused. You've always known what to do, what's a good plan, Sis? What should I do when nothing is what I think?

Love,

Alison

My phone beeped. Message from Alison, the screen screamed.

Despite many reservations, I wanted to put the past behind me. But what was the use of bearing resentment over what had gone wrong and what might have been when the present was here right now?

Her text message was concise.

'Let's start again. Maybe I owe you a meal. Want to meet up? What are you doing this weekend? Alison.'

How could I refuse this sorceress? And yes, I desperately wanted to see her again if only to set the record straight, or at least that's what I told myself. After all, we'd seen each other in our most vulnerable states. Stark bloody naked! Doesn't everyone deserve a second chance?

'Sunday's clear. Time and place? Jamie.'

Her reply came back at the speed of light. *'Pick up at your place early seven am, OK? Ali.'*

All this gave me several days to contemplate what I had got myself into. That I knew she was amoral went without saying. Maybe she had turned a new leaf. I was about to find out.

When her little silver Mazda 2 pulled up outside, it was barely dawn; the sun was still deciding whether to rise from its nightly bed, something I could relate to. What was I getting myself into?

'Hi.'

'Throw your things on the back seat, we've got a bit of a drive.'

Over the next few minutes I learnt she was taking me home, some two hours out in the country. There Alison had grown up with her parents and sisters on a farm raising sheep and growing grain. For high school she had boarded in the city returning home every term holidays until uni beckoned.

By now we were zooming along, the city vanished behind us, the kilometres clicking by, the scenery blurry. Could she be a serial killer taking me to her latest killing field? I wondered. Best I engage her in conversation.

'Listen, Alison, I have an early morning shift tomorrow, we'll have to come back tonight.'

'Fine by me. You can drive us, I'm not so good at night-time,' she said.

Despite my memories I nodded.

'What were you studying at uni?' I said.

'Science,' she said.

'Right,' I said. 'Any particular stream?'

'Laboratory science.'

'Oh, medical or forensic?'

'Somewhere in between. Reproductive. IVF.'

I gulped. That'd be right. Uni for the theory, my house for the prac, her baby the course result. Oh my God, she'd done her entire course on her back. Still, hadn't I pledged not to bear grudges? Move on, Jamie, I said to myself.

'Your baby?'

'Oh, Arnold. The story of his life is on the back seat.'

Twisting around, one hand accidentally gripped her leg, my other a leather bound book, "How orgasm can improve fertility rates," glared back at me. Right! I looked out the window at the road signs.

'To create life, what a thrill,' she said, pausing, 'Leave your hand there, Jamie, I don't mind.'

An hour into the journey my male bladder called, half an hour further it yelled.

'Sorry, could you pull over? Yeah, there's a decent tree, Alison, that'll do.'

Phew, what a relief.

'Thanks for stopping, up to the gills, you know how it is.'

She smiled, the same cheeky smile I remembered from my bathroom. Without conscious thought I leant over and kissed her. A quick thank you sort of kiss, that's all it started off as. The engine stalled. She hesitated for a moment then pulled me back for more. What a kisser. That's when I knew I was definitely heading into unknown territory. Boy, she had passion and technique, but then, as her latest victim, what did I expect?

'Ah, that's better. Let's keep going or we'll never get there,' she said, a coy note in her voice.

I agreed.

More and more houses popped up like spring mushrooms as we were approaching the outskirts of a country town, Alison cleared her throat.

'I should warn you, Jamie love, my family doesn't hold back much,' she said. 'We're a very close family with few secrets. Everyone's very, well, frank.'

'Right,' I shuddered. What else did this family know? Were they aware of the Alison I knew?

'But,' she continued, 'you can speak your mind freely, no one takes offence, just be prepared to argue your point.'

'And we are ...?' I intoned.

The town 60 km limit sign appeared. We slowed.

'What do you want us to be?' she posed.

I slunk further into the seat and prepared to meet my fate.

After she was greeted like a saint by sisters, brothers-in-law and her mother, Ali introduced me to the latest addition to the family, a baby I had last seen in a pram and her elder sister's proudest acquisition. Sister's? Little Arnold was always surrounded by someone, an IVF miracle, they said, whose positing, poohing, weeing and every bit of wind was greeted with excitement. IVF? Ben, the father, was like a dog with two tails. Here was a family where unconditional love ruled. After a bit I excused ourselves and led Ali out for some fresh air and a walk. I wanted to see where she had grown up and she was keen to show me. It felt as if I was exploring Mars, that's how foreign it was. Everything seemed surreal. If there was something keeping me grounded it was Alison's hand in mine. Feelings I thought were submerged in that bath scene surfaced like she had. How could I help being entranced?

'Alison,' I started, pulling her to a stop.

'Yup.'

'I want you to know I realise what you got up to at night and that I'm fine with it, alright?'

'Good,' she said, her arms pulling me close, 'I'm glad to hear it. Those recordings for my IVF thesis must have driven you crazy. Let's go in for tea. You're sitting next to me.'

Recordings? IVF again? What was she talking about? Thesis? Had I missed more vital clues about her nocturnal activities?

At the end of the main course, apparently it was a family tradition to take a conversation break before sweets. Maybe they were curious as to how Alison and I fitted together; it seemed I was considered somewhat of a mystery to them. I wondered which inquisitor would ask the crucial questions. Alison's oldest sister, Sis, reached over to clear the plates away whilst I was still chewing on my last mouthful.

'So Jamie, you and Alison seem to be getting on well. Must have a common interest, music perhaps? But what're your thoughts on the clitoris and the female orgasm?'

My food sprayed across the table, some catching in the throat. Alison leant over and thumped my back.

'Jamie's more of an expert with illegal drugs, not sex, Sis,' she said. 'So far.'

My dad, the Greenie

(Or 'How our Father Tried to Save the World, but Nearly Killed us Doing so.' Written by a family survivor.)

Our father was a born-again environmentalist. No, not an evangelist, an environmentalist, although he always approached the subject of climate change with a similar, almost religious zeal. Never did he tackle issues close to his heart with anything less than single-minded fervour. My cuddly, indefatigable dad believed that if everyone started changing things at an individual level, the world would soon be saved. He saw it as his mission to lead by example. That was my dad.

Even when Dad was young he was a hyper-active member of the Green Corps, a somewhat fanatical group devoted to saving the world from itself, although I did overhear him once saying in an aside to our neighbour that it was a great place to pull birds. Even later I found out that he was not referring to some virtuous ornithological practice, but was making an attempt at seducing naïve females. How disgusting!

Dad said he found Mum at a rubbish dump, to our embarrassment something she never denied. Apparently she'd backed her own father's trailer of prunings right over the tipping edge, the trailer dangling down behind the car like a giant hanging basket, and of course my gallant dad came to the rescue. It had nothing to do with the hot summer weather and the fact that she was wearing a bikini, but because they were both dedicated environmentalists working at the cutting edge, or so he recounted with a sly grin. Apparently they had attended the same protest meetings and shared a common concern for minimalist living; both were broke uni students at the time. Mum later confidentially told me she wanted to borrow her father's car to go out on a hot date, but had to empty the trailer first. I sometimes wondered what that other guy would have been like as a father instead of Dad. Fate's funny, isn't it? In an earlier time my parents would have been classed as 60's hippies, certainly they wore little clothing between the bathroom and bedroom at night time. Minimalist living? Sorry, too much information.

And so my siblings and I grew up clothed in hand-me-downs and living in a humble household furnished with second-hand recycled everything. 'Preloved' was king, we never knew anything else. Dad said 'new' was a four letter word, work that out! Outside was similarly cluttered with electrical items that just needed another one in order to be fixable. Fair enough to use washable cloth nappies rather than disposables, but did Dad have to take me out for fresh air in a wheelbarrow rather than a pram? As soon as I could walk by myself I did. Shame is a great motivator.

When he brought in an 'unloved' playmate for me to play with, I failed to see the point. The boy, a new kid from next door, had been standing looking forlornly down the driveway at our old trampoline, scrounged off one verge collection or another. The rusty old trampoline, a magnet for kids in our neighbourhood, had only needed a couple of bolts, new springs and mat. It was a real gift, according to Dad. He had taken pity on the kid, 'Better come in son,' he'd said. Actually I think the parents were very understanding about Dad's afternoon abduction later that night. Fortunately, they'd delayed ringing the police as the father was the latest cop assigned to the area. More about that kid later.

Timed showers, impromptu talks about leaving lights on unnecessarily and becoming self sufficient in vegetable growing were all part of our youth. Waste was a fate worse than death with 'materialism the modern evil' that was destroying the earth as we knew it, they said. Really? However, saving the planet also came with extreme humiliation. When my dad turned up at my best friend's 12th birthday party on a tandem bike, second-hand of course, to bring me home I could have cheerfully strangled him. 'Non-polluting transport,' he proclaimed proudly, 'how many fathers can say that?' Who would want to, I fumed. But when he installed an old phone book in the toilet for use as toilet paper, even Mum gave an uncomfortable grimace, and that was before she used the shiny, black ink laden paper! By this time everyone's bum was now permanently stained. No way could I bring anyone home with Dad's strange 'green' economies. Absolutely not! We washed our clothes in an old-fashioned copper, the dishes in a large plastic bowl and emptied the water directly onto the garden ourselves. Grey water? We took credit for creating the term; of course it helped that this was our surname.

Dad's name was Hugh Grey, a name which gave rise to many family jokes. 'Hugh (who) done it' and 'Hugh's (who's) been here', were some. When someone did a new 'Hugherism', he'd just throw back his head and laugh. 'Hugh's laughing now,' he'd say. Mum's name was Penelope, which got shortened to Penny, but for some strange reason he never made any wise cracks about that, once saying she wore the pants in the family, another phrase that took years to decipher. Didn't everyone wear pants, I asked him at the time. He just smiled back, pulled me close and tousled my hair. Hmm.

Dad's environmentalist energy took a severe dent when he was threatened with arrest one Sunday. How was he possibly to know the guy was only emptying the catcher and not leaving the unattended mower on the verge for collection? We all agreed it was a mistake that anyone could have made. Fortunate that the police officer next door was a recent recruit in Dad's footy team and let him off with a warning. The fine was a carton of beer, but in reality he was just another friend for Dad.

Come to think of it, the whole family became organic farmers before it was fashionable. Dad always made weird nocturnal visits to the backyard lemon tree, ostensibly for 'watering' purposes. Communing with nature, he'd say, whilst zipping up his pants afterwards. Was that why the lemons were so acidic? I wondered. But then again Mum was an avid composter with all the vegie scraps finding their way into an old hinged 44 gallon drum down the back. You should have seen the strange mushrooms that grew inside, ones that we weren't meant to mention.

'Helps one imagine the scene,' she said.

To me her paintings still looked like psychedelic nightmares, although not to Dad, who saw Mum as an unrecognised artistic genius. My brother even took to growing plants in pots, although I never did establish exactly what species of kitchen 'herbs' had such weird spiky shaped leaves. Next, my sister insisted on pets, so Mum and Dad let her have chickens as long as we got eggs from them. And for me, well, I became a vegan, except on two nights a week when Mum insisted I have red meat to bolster my blood, a girly thing, she said. She had experimented with homeopathic herbs as replacement for the contraceptive pill after marriage but had given up when I, and then my two siblings, appeared. Apparently Dad's spermatozoa were too strong for the herbs, she said. Had she got her herbs confused with Horny Goat Weed? I wondered. Way too much information.

The family's pride and joy took physical root however, when we gained possession of a car. Not just any car mind, but a diesel. Buying a car was a major concession for Dad's green ethics. But it took nearly an hour to ride his bike each day to work and he'd had several near misses on the busy roads, something we all worried about. Despite his green eccentricities we loved him unconditionally. Sort of, that is.

'Hugh's going to be doing what with that rust bucket?' Mum asked when the 80's Holden Gemini pulled up in the driveway with a screech of brakes, knocking the rubbish bin over.

Unlicensed, unroadworthy and unkempt, the car surely represented all that was wrong with what our parents had been preaching about modern consumer society.

'Free fuel, dear,' Dad answered patiently, tapping the side of his nose, 'it'll run on the smell of an oily rag, literally. Used cooking oil, you know? Pay for itself in a couple of years, just be patient, alright?'

Oh yeah, our beloved paternal had read a magazine article on biodiesel and decided to jump on the oil burner bandwagon. There appeared to be only three drawbacks: everyone else had cottoned onto the lurk so old cooking oil was hard to source; the car wouldn't start in cold weather when the oil solidified, and worst was that we drove around with a legion of barking and salivating dogs behind so everyone knew when we were coming. The car's exhaust stank like a Chinese restaurant. After all, that's where Dad got the oil.

'Good bloke that Chan,' Dad said, 'if we buy a meal there each week he'll give us the oil for free.'

I wondered about the logic, especially when Dad was still forced into riding his bike during winter.

Our next venture in practical environmentalism was solar power. Through an ingenious system of roof panels, a spaghetti collection of wires under every carpet and a bedroom filled with banks of old car batteries, Dad transformed our house into a gem of energy efficiency. He even turned off the gas and electricity at the meter box just in case we weakened and went back to non-renewable energy. If the oceans rose and everyone got wet feet it wouldn't be due to us, he boasted.

'I'm proud of you Hugh,' said Mum, squinting in the gloom, 'but aren't the lights a bit dim these days?'

'Depends on the sun. Maybe it's your eyes, Penny dear,' he replied, 'maybe you need glasses at your age.'

I'm sure he didn't see her hackles rise and I wondered if he wasn't the one who needed glasses.

Hot showers became distant memories, the house got darker and colder with winter so I did my homework by flickering candlelight while we dressed like Neanderthal cavemen to ward off the cold. Climate change? Not in our 'green' household.

Relief came unexpectedly in the shape of a storm. With the Weather Bureau predicting gale force winds and warning householders to secure loose items outside, we battened down the hatches and retired to bed early. It was warmer snuggled under the old moth-eaten woollen blankets anyway.

The loud crash and sound of breaking glass during the evening got everyone wondering but sleep overtook us until morning. With the light of day, Dad wandered around in his saggy, baggy pyjamas to see what damage the storm had wreaked. Our solar plant had failed that morning but Dad put it down to the heavy cloud cover. However, next door our neighbour's new car was sporting what appeared to be the remains of our solar panels, something that promised to impress them little. Dad quickly and quietly slipped back inside on the auspices of getting dressed whilst summoning up the courage to break the news to Mum. Later on, promising to make amends to the neighbours, we carted the broken panels back home as roofing for the chooks. Why Dad hadn't screwed the panels down I'll never know, but I wondered if anything else around our household wasn't screw-loose.

'I've got it, love, wind power,' Dad said next, with all the optimism of a born-again environmentalist, 'why didn't I think of that before?'

Mum was sporting her new expensive multi-focal glasses but they didn't fully disguise an exasperated look. With muted optimism that only an older greenie could possess, Mum decreed that any future projects had to be cost-neutral. The bank account was empty and the bank manager getting restless. After a few uncomfortable nights alone on our lounge sofa, her lover and husband, our father, reluctantly agreed. Fortunately, we kids all used earplugs on our secret iPods and couldn't hear them 'reconciling' that night.

Following the cooking oil fiasco, Dad decided to experiment with ethanol.

'Fuel of the future,' he said confidentially, adding, 'should have thought of it earlier. Oil's getting expensive, did you see the prices on Chan's menu last night? Costing us a fortune. Yep, it's ethanol we need.'

With all the fervour that only a committed tree-hugger could muster, Dad raided the streets near and far during the next verge collection, bringing home the biggest assortment of strange vessels ever seen. Cost neutral, hell, you could hardly see the backyard lawn for worthless junk. Weekends went by when the only sign that our father existed was from the hammering, drilling and sawing sounds emanating from his shed. He had also conned Mum into buying extra bulk chook feed from the farmers' supply shop – all of us were intrigued with what he was going to make. And how it would affect us.

Finally, the tempo of Dad's efforts lessened and a sly grin developed on his face at tea-time. This could only mean one of two things, the promise of another marital 'reconciliation' or a successful backyard enterprise.

'Got a bit of a surprise for everyone tomorrow,' he announced. They were indeed ominous words.

All of us 'greenified' siblings looked at one another for clues; each shook our heads, there were none.

'Could be on a winner, kids. People are going to remember me for this.'

How true it was.

When our illustrious male parent failed to appear at tea-time the next night, Mum sent me down the backyard to investigate. Sprawled across the old large carpet on the workshop floor my father laid like a corpse but with his eyes slowly opening and closing, a beatific grin on his face.

'Dad, Dad, are you OK?' I yelled, kneeling down and wondering what had happened. Despite everything we loved our dad and didn't want to lose him, although there were times Mum's eyes took on an especially despairing look. Her world was yet to be saved.

'Neber besher, sweshheart. Old legs gone a bish wobbly on me,' he said and hiccupped.

From all I could remember from my first aid classes, Dad had either had a stroke or was drunk. But how could he be drunk? There were no telltale bottles littering the workshop benches, only an over-powering chemical stench emanating from his workshop contraption merrily boiling away. Gradually, it dawned on me over the roar of the old BBQ burner and trickling of liquids into cans that Dad had constructed a still, a distillery unit. Aha, so that was his project. And wasn't ethanol a form of alcohol – he had inhaled the fumes and gotten himself pissed. Just like me and the policeman's son from next door on a bottle of Dad's home brew when he tried to kiss me whilst examining my growing breasts and I let him. Where was Troy now, I wondered. Nice French kisser, too, all at a time when I thought the tongue was only for eating. Wanted to be a cop like his dad I seem to recall. Hadn't exactly been a queue of guys lining up since, either. Oh well.

Mum, along with the rest of us, didn't know whether to laugh or cry. In the end, the family consensus decided on mild hysterics, especially whilst Dad was safely out of it. It also made carrying his supine body up to the house easier, each of us attached to a limb. In no fit state to complain about our rough handling, indeed his snores and incoherent mumbling meant he could feel no pain. Yet.

Tea that night was quite a strange affair with Dad sleeping it off in his bedroom. Occasionally, one of us kids would begin sniggering, Mum would vainly try chastising, then off we'd go into laughter again.

As a special treat we were allowed to turn on the TV early that night, but halfway through our favourite program came the biggest explosion we'd ever heard. It was truly remarkable in its loudness and closeness; exceptionally loud and exceptionally close. The tremendous bang also triggered a fascinating response in Mum, the first time I'd ever heard her swear.

'Shit, what was that? Did Hugh hear that?'

The answer came in another form about 30 seconds later as 'that' became a rain of metal descending on our house's tin roof. It sounded like a cross between a gunnery range and fireworks. All of us instinctively ducked until the barrage ceased. Outside, Dad's shed had mysteriously disappeared and its contents were lying scattered around the fence line, leaving a pervading brewery aroma. Inside the bedroom, Dad slept right through the noise and chorus of barking neighbourhood dogs. Typical. He'd always dozed through many of the important events in her life, according to Mum. Hmm.

It was only when the Council Security Ute pulled up behind the fire engine that was alongside the police car, that the second sign of strain on Mum's face emerged. Or maybe it was the street full of somewhat deafened neighbours all standing outside our place and shouting to one another in a confused fashion. Hard to say which affected her more.

'Hugh's your bloody father?' she ranted to us kids, as a startled fireman looked on, amazed at the passion in her words, 'and when he sobers up, I'm going to bloody kill Hugh.'

The police glanced at one another, deciding whether to arrest Dad for being drunk or Mum for using threatening language. Fortunately, she played basketball with one of the cop's wives. Apparently they'd heard about Dad's commitment to saving the world. Oh right, I thought, now we had acquired a public reputation as greenie loonies. And was there any doubt about my parentage, I sincerely hoped so.

Eventually peace returned to our otherwise quiet neighbourhood when the flashing red, blue and amber lights eventually faded down the street. Everyone went back inside as the last of the glazier's vans left. They'd made a weekend overtime killing, replacing the shattered panes of glass in people's windows, something Mum had promised to pay for, somehow, sometime. We had yet to fix up the 'solar-powered' problem from the storm with the neighbour next door! Along with the remnants of any social standing went my brother's weird pot plants into the police van. It took ages to clean up the place, so Mum hired a rubbish skip and into it went all the now unwanted, accumulated items waiting for a second life.

Old pots, newspapers, bikes, wood, fridges, TV's and washing machines. Our house almost looked tidy again. Green it wasn't, unusually neat it was.

Mum and Dad eventually reconciled their temporary difficulties and life went on, but not quite as before. They had to pick up a lot of extra work to account for their earlier 'ecological savings' so both had little energy to waste on arguing about what had happened and who was to blame. I was impressed at their dedication to saving the environment, not everyone would have done what they did. Thank Heavens.

Time moved on and it was some years later that Dad's next environmental venture provided nearly everyone with a sense of wonder. Even he wasn't sure it would work. Borrowing the neighbour's lawn mower, the ones on the upwind side that couldn't smell the grass-eating goat and whose car hadn't gone 'solar', Dad set up base camp outside our bathroom window. 'Sewer gas,' he said to me conspiratorially, 'fuel of the future. Methane, cleanest burning gas known.'

I was home from uni for the weekend and Dad had roped me into giving him a hand. Mum unknowingly donated her vacuum cleaner's flexible hose, not that this was a great sacrifice. Didn't she hate vacuuming household spiders and cute daddy longlegs? Somehow it seemed a unique excuse for avoiding housework, not that we kids ever volunteered ourselves. Environmental sensitivity, no. Laziness, yes.

Our paternal soon installed the mower on top of an old dented 44 gallon drum, the concertinaed vacuum cleaner hose coming down from the toilet vent on the roof and sitting next to the mower's air cleaner. Even with the mower vibrating on top of the drum, an almost visionary gleam came to Dad's eyes. The definitive experiment was about to begin.

My job was to stop the mower falling down, no easy task with it anxious to take off at any minute and cut everything but grass in its path, like me. Dad gave the mower a few revs, then reached somewhere underneath to turn off the petrol tap. All this whilst holding the vacuum cleaner hose close by at the ready. As the engine began to run out of petrol, he slipped the hose onto the air cleaner. No one was more amazed than I when the mower picked up and kept running, this time on sewer gas. The triumphant look on Dad's face was priceless, for once he had been vindicated. Wow! Even I was impressed. Methane and free energy! He had in mind that the next version would have been a generator set running outside the bathroom all courtesy of our toilet's methane, something my flatulent brother was never short of. It seemed that all my father's birthdays had come at once. I was immensely proud of his perseverance when all else in the world had appeared to be conspiring against him. Despite everything, Dad had saved the world, and he was my dad. How proud was his daughter, and I basked in the sunshine of his success. 'Hugh' was a genius! How I loved my dad, the fruit of his loins.

What exactly happened next I'm not sure, but the mower suddenly backfired, an errant blue flame shot up the hose from the air cleaner, then an instant later there was a muffled boom from inside the house. Dad's face clouded over in confusion, but not before someone gave a huge yell from the other side of the bathroom wall. Mum! Next she scuttled out through the back door, her knickers draped around her ankles and dripping what appeared to be water everywhere. I swear I never knew she was in there, well, not really.

'Hugh's done it again, what the hell's going on now?' she bellowed. 'Just wait until I catch you, you bloody Greenie! Always trying to get my pants down.'

Dad took off down one side of the house and it seemed a good time to beat a quick retreat around the other, somewhere

I could be out of sight and give relief to my mirth. Shit, that was funny, I never knew Mum's bum looked like that, as white as two giant co-joined marshmallows. We kids all got sore stomachs laughing at the sight, for once not a result of her vegan cooking.

Mum and Dad eventually reconciled their difficulties yet again, albeit very slowly, and life continued, but not before she made him pay her back for the new mower, join the local bowling club and give his green credentials a well-earned rest. He'd burnt his last eco-bridge with Mum. Finally. And he knew it.

'Hey, sweetheart, I met someone whilst at the police station the other day,' he began, looking at me. 'Just broken up with his girlfriend, looks like a nice guy too. Thought you might be interested.'
He placed a slip of paper with a phone number onto the table in front of me. My mouth opened of its own accord in amazement. What? So Dad was now into recycling people. Not content with once trying to save the planet's ecology, he saw his new mission to match second-hand people together. Me with a criminal? As if.

'What do you take me for, desperate?' I retorted, quietly palming the paper scrap. Oh, Troy, him, well, maybe. My boobs were bigger than when I was 15 but maybe he'd now notice the person behind them.

Sometime later Mum began to worry again when Dad took to the streets on his bike most weekends, supposedly under the guise of exercise, or was it a mid-life crisis? Whilst first she worried he was having a clandestine affair, actually he had discovered garage sales, his purchases being carried home very furtively under the disguise of darkness. But it was his obsession with the Internet that made Mum the most suspicious, especially when his computer searches covered everything 'atomic' between Hiroshima to Chernobyl, Long Island onto Fukoshima. Bugger!

In the interests of family harmony I paid a friendly visit to Dad in his reconstructed shed, now heavily fortified and kept locked, apparently due to National Security concerns, or so he said. While some of the equipment was hidden under an old tarpaulin, I did recognise an enormous drum of ex-army luminous paint, heavy rolls of lead sheeting, the Gemini's gearbox, several bags of fertiliser, some quarry detonators and a Second World War Geiger counter. My eyes widened.

'Nuclear power, sweetheart,' he said to me conspiratorially, 'I may have solved the instantaneous chain reaction problem, I'll use gears to slow it down instead. No greenhouse gases, see. Could make a big impact on the environment and put the country on the map for once. What could possibly go wrong, I ask you?'

With my wedding planned for a month's time, I shuddered. Would we all survive Dad's heartfelt concern for the world? Back in the kitchen Mum agreed with my reservations before a revengeful glint slowly came to her eyes and she asked that I leave the problem in her hands.

'What would Hugh know?' she said with a mother to daughter wink.

Thank Heavens. Where would we be without our mums? In her I trusted.

Between Mum's furtive trips to one of her basketball girls, a hairdresser, and the chemist, the family went quietly about its business. At the meal table I wondered out loud whether Dad's hair was thinning while a generous dose of laxative secretively found its way into his every drink. Dad was forced to get his priorities right and soon put his shed project on temporary hold, spending most of his time sitting astride the toilet and staring nervously at his hair laden comb and blocked shower drain. Peeking through the doorway, the parental bedroom and bathroom looked more like the floor of a shearer's shed strewn with grey coloured wool.

It was my wedding day and Dad seemed unusually jumpy, waddling down the church aisle alongside me, his buttocks tightly squeezed together, a walk not unlike Charlie Chaplin. I hoped Mum had reduced his dose so he could get through the service without his old 'op shop' pin-striped blue trousers turning brown. In honour of the occasion my brother had been specially let out on parole following his arrest at a mate's hydroponic herb farm. Whilst we thought he had been doing a special horticultural course, his excuse was that marijuana had hidden medicinal qualities, if only he could stay awake long enough and remember what they were. My little sister, Sophie, was my bridesmaid with hibiscus flowers behind her ears, a roll of 'back-up' toilet paper subtly hidden under the bouquet. Thanks, Soph, I love ya.

'Sweetheart, I need to know something, it's urgent,' Dad whispered into my ear.

Stopped, we were only halfway down the aisle as his reddened eyes, probably due to the lack of sleep, peered anxiously at me. Everyone in the congregation looked on, wondering if I had developed cold feet.

'What?' I whispered back. This was no time for him to have reservations. Had he discovered what Troy and I had been getting up to in my bedroom before the wedding? With his policeman-inquisitive hands, no way! Full body and cavity search in private, yes, please.

'I'm going to abandon that last project; the world will have to cope without me. What do you know about radioactivity?' Dad asked, his eyes pleading for reassurance.

'Love you Dad,' I said, warmly kissing his cheek and half-dragging him up the aisle.

And that's how I ended up with a cop for a husband, someone else I love to bits. He saves the world, but not by being a 'Greenie'!

Transumerism

(or 'Why Buy When You Can Hire?')

' ... and the taking of recreational drugs or sex is strictly forbidden ...'

'I should hope so.'

'... that is initiated by the client,' added the crisp, secretarial voice on the phone.

'Oh.'

'Ours is a professional partnering service, Ms Ainslie, not a dating or escort service,' she continued brusquely. 'All our partners are fully trained and come with police clearance. Absolute discretion, anonymity and confidentiality assured, satisfaction guaranteed. The all inclusive fee is $350, very reasonable with such late notice.'

I went to protest but stopped myself. If only it wasn't so important to portray a certain 'stable' image to the state advertising body, the conference dinner group could go hang and I would attend unescorted. Unfortunately, reputation, ambition and promotion usually went hand in hand, or so my boss hinted.

'And should your partner be required to perform a speech, it will incur an additional charge. I trust all that is acceptable,' finally she finished her spiel.

I agreed.

So after giving my credit card details along with the evening's arrangements, I considered myself fortunate to have so conveniently solved a problem. What did we do when male company was required before the Internet? Should every woman have to wait to be asked out, then put up with boozy, indulgent thoughts and wandering hands? No, not now, I was a modern, independent and empowered woman, mistress of my own destiny. Or so I thought.

OK, my job embodied me. Why buy when you can hire?

At the other end of a phone line a screen glowed as a hoarse cough drowned out the click of his computer mouse. It was a week later.

'S-s-shit, I've got a booking tonight,' Wayne said.

'Turn off the light when you come home this time,' his older brother and flatmate reminded him. 'The power bill's gone through the roof lately.'

'N-n-no, it's serious. I can't go, you can see that, you b-b-blind b-b-bastard, this flu has knocked me for s-s-six.'

'Then ring in sick.'

'And lose my job, n-n-no, not an option.'

After Stripagrams, the 'Partnering' service was proving better paid. How else could he work his way through uni?

'There's nothing else for it; you'll have to go in my place. It's only a conference dinner anyway. Four hours tops, taxi there and back, all snug in bed before midnight.'

An exasperated sigh signified reluctant consideration.

'It's not my scene having to make polite conversation with spoilt bitches all night as well as all day. High maintenance women, who needs them? Surely there's more to life than appearances?'

'L-l-listen mate, you can have the entire fee, alright? $200's not bad for a night's work, meal and drinks included. S-s-sometimes you can even get lucky, desperate w-w-women, you know what I mean?'

'If it is considered a one-off then.'

His brother passed on the arrangements, adding, 'O-o-only one thing bro, don't use your real name. Just a precaution in case you get a s-s-stalker, OK?'

From my side-on perspective, my dinner partner surpassed everything the agency promised. Immaculately neat in an Armani suit not out of place amid the professional offices in West Perth. Givenchy aftershave? Late 20's or early 30's, if only he wouldn't keep looking at his Rolex watch. With no obvious piercings, tats or noisy bodily functions, I was deeply impressed with my choice of hire. Wow! At one stage I caught him examining my face intensely.

'Simply perfect,' he said, gently trailing his long fingers down my face from forehead to neck.

A pubescent schoolgirl could not have blushed more. When I challenged his scrutiny, he gently turned my hand over, almost in what I wondered was to be a romantic fashion.

'Good veins,' he said.

For a moment I contemplated whether he was a drug enforcement agent looking for needle tracks. Either way I found my partner fascinating. A wry grin that escaped when he thought I wasn't noticing hid another persona lurking underneath, of that I was sure. Oh yeah, what a spunk.

'So, Emile, what do you do when you're not ...?'

'Reconstruction repairs,' he answered, 'What else?'

My brow wrinkled before I wondered if he was pulling my leg. Emile, a builder with those unblemished hands?

I laughed out loud. 'No, what's your real job, I'm interested.'

Maybe he meant a renovation architect, as in house restoration.

For a moment he hesitated. 'Same as yours, pandering to other people's vanity.'

It was a thought-provoking reply since I worked in advertising, my latest project being 'Transumerism'. Research had shown that, with experience being one of the cornerstones of happiness, people were more likely to hire immediate pleasure these days rather than save up forever in a vain attempt to gain possession. With holiday and equipment rentals going ballistic, I was spearheading national advertising campaigns selling instantaneous gratification. No maintenance, no commitment, how could I go wrong? Charter, lease, contract. Why buy much later when you can hire now, I was a living example. My professional career was assured.

The remainder of the evening went pleasantly enough, I had to admit. My dinner partner was seriously good at making conversation and discerning eye contact with every woman at the meal table. It was as though he saw everyone as a potential client for a house renovation. One of my bosses' wives even thought she knew him, something he slyly discounted with a cheeky grin. OK, my emotions were being incrementally kidnapped.

Once, I caught his leg lightly resting against mine and, in his company, time flew by. And if the evening hadn't been a business arrangement, I wondered if Emile might have liked me as much as I was attracted to him. Then, with midnight coming, the band announced one last number.

'Come on Tegan, time for one quick spin around the floor,' he said extending his hand.

Then, possibly due to my translucent silk dress and synthetic indoor grass, a tiny electrostatic spark flew between us.

'Ow,' I laughed.

'That's something you should do a lot more often,' Emile grinned back.

The music transported us away to a world where only the two of us existed, or so I thought; a place where his hands encompassed me like an octopus, one hand high on my shoulder, one hand low on my waist or had it somehow slipped? Such nimble fingered hands too. Did I mind, no way, not in this deal. Business aside, could we not have another dance, pretty please?

When the hired taxi pulled up outside my apartment, I paid the fare and, without thinking, asked Emile in. The most obscure aura about him intrigued me; I sensed mystery, emotion and hidden depths, something I loved about a man. There was more to know about Emile, of this was sure. Maybe I should have hired him for longer. How would some of my preconceived ideas of modern men stack up against him, I wanted to know. Prepare for the inquisition, Emile, I thought. Coffee, then a quick kiss and cuddle if he passed.

'Against the rules, but thanks anyway. Goodnight,' he said leaning over dismissively past me, my lips pursed for his kiss, to give the driver another address.

Bloody smartarse, I thought to myself, wondering what on earth had made me consider such an invitation anyway. Coffee and conversation was all that I had in mind, didn't he realise that I wasn't that desperate? Well, not really.

A smell of rotten egg gas from the swiftly departing taxi's exhaust was my last memory of the evening. And with not even a quick peck on my cheek, I felt cheated, short changed even. Get stuffed Emile, I thought, if that's the way you want it. Don't you know this girl rents not buys? Commitment, no way.

No sooner had the new financial year begun but another wretched email invitation arrived; this time from my old secondary college Year 12 group celebrating a ten year reunion or something similarly disconcerting. Inwardly I groaned. Weren't reunions only another chance for my old school mates to gloat over their successful marriages and prodigy children, something of which I had neither. Then a thought crossed my mind, eight clicks of my laptop mouse and the problem was solved. They wouldn't know what hit them. Of course. Professionalpartners.com. Wasn't a non-committal night's $350 cheap compared to an expensive multi-million divorce? Why be obliged to buy when you can hire?

When the swarthy taxi driver turned up with a turnip-faced passenger looking out at me expectantly, I wondered what the hell was going on. Hadn't I requested my previous partner from last time? Emile?

'Where's Emile?' were my first words. We had unfinished business.

'W-w-who? Oh, you must mean the other guy. H-h-he's, he's unavailable,' my evening's partner, Wayne, stammered, the first faux pas of the evening.

OK, maybe I shouldn't have tried to pass off my hired partner as a husband of five years and father of three genius kids. I despaired as Wayne woefully stammered and stuttered his way through the evening of cold party pies, sausage rolls and warm light beer. Even the dumbest person in my class year sussed out our fake act. The guys talked football, leaving me to endure all the girls discussing nappies, breastfeeding and comparing the interest rate on their family home's mortgage. At least they all left early to relieve their babysitters, whereas I left in humiliation with my tail between my legs. They had love coming out their ears but, apart from a successful career, what did I have? What sort of company did a leased laptop provide in a rented flat when it got dark and cold outside? Doubt crept in about transumerism. Phone on monthly contract, my job on casual rates, so why did I feel incomplete? Temporary versus permanent. Flexi-time defying fixed award hours. How did I defend against the appeal of someone like my Emile?

'H-h-h-hope you enjoyed the evening,' Wayne intoned, 'C-c-coffee?'

His hint was as subtle as his bad breath and pervasive BO.

'In your dreams,' I replied, heading inside.

I was learning that renting came with risks.

Despite my indignation when I rang the agency to complain, no way would the old agency buzzard release any personal information, nor accept that an 'Emile' worked for her anyway. 'Weren't you told the partnering service was confidential?' was her patronising response. For once in my 29 years I was stymied and it hurt. Shit.

Normally, the social section in the newspaper interested me little, but this particular week's social column of local identities parading in evening dress caught my eye as I flicked through to the financial pages. A familiar face with hands somewhat entwined around a leggy, over-endowed society butterfly peered back at me; her permanently fixed

Botox grin and wide-eyed face would have been more at home in Hollywood. Mutton dressed as lamb was probably a more apt description. His name, however, was not Emile at all; it was Marcel Popovich, a plastic surgeon allegedly famous for wrinkle removal and boob enhancement. Not for nothing was he facetiously known as the 'breast surgeon of Dalkeith'. I gulped, so my partner Emile really did have hidden talents. But in my vengeful mind he was long overdue for his comeuppance; I wondered what the paper would have made of him masquerading as a male escort. But what was a plastic surgeon doing moonlighting as a high class escort when he could be earning a squillion dollars promoting mass immunisation by Botox injection and straightening every snobbish nose in town? Emile, or Marcel, whoever you bloody are, where are you?

In the end, though, some deeper research discovered another side of my dinner partner, a side not exposed for public viewing. A friend's daughter who worked as a nurse at the central hospital confirmed my Google search that even Marcel was not all he seemed. Masked and cloaked in green gowns, Marcel, alias my Emile, moonlighted in pro bono facial reconstruction of cleft palate defects amongst children from third world countries. I just knew it; this was a guy I wanted to see a lot more of. Was he available, was he interested, these questions plagued me like an Indian telemarketer. I aimed my sights and hoped like crazy.

Getting an appointment proved tricky. Did I give up? No way was my professional reputation for tenacity going to be tarnished by a phony escort. In the end a fake West Perth doctor's reference, not too difficult with our office scanner and printer, got me as far as his Nazi secretary. Then a personal plea for bodily perfection, combined with my credit card details of course, finally gained me a date and time.

'Ah, Ms Ainslie,' he intoned, his eyes never leaving the

computer screen in front of him. 'What can I do for you? Facial, breast, bum or tummy?'

'A truth transplant and enhancement,' I smiled sweetly, tongue firmly-in-cheek.

'Oh right, not a problem, what size did you have in mind?' he said, tapping away at the keyboard before glancing up as the words dawned on him. Finally I had his attention. 'But don't I know you? Tegan? What are you doing here?'

I took the initiative. 'Satisfaction guaranteed, I was told, Emile, or is it Marcel today, otherwise I want my money back.'

He grinned, the same mischievous grin that had entranced me before. 'Can I take you out in compensation, my shout?' His hand gently covered mine.

'I'd like that.'

Why hire when you want a life membership?

Not What it Seems

So many memories flood back, just like an incoming tide, each memory a rippling wave over the one before. Like how I ended up in prison, an innocent person, something that most here also believe of themselves. How could it have happened? Oh ... yes.

Life is not always what it seems.

'He's got charisma, heaps of money and takes me places,' my ex had crowed with red lip gloss glistening, the fake Chanel 10 I'd mistakenly bought, thinking it was as real as my feelings, filling the air like fly spray. Whatever had I seen in her?

Through the distorted haze of a beer glass I contemplated life, one that made me question many things. Like why didn't I have more money, charisma and someone in my life who saw me as interesting, maybe even lovable? Alright, someone who needed me in their life, who couldn't live without me. At 31, all I had going for me was my mechanic's ticket and an almost photographic memory, a gift that'd always proved useful for remembering specifications, car identification, registrations and people's features.

Our dealership catered primarily for the rich; social snobs who saw their car as a status symbol. The fact that we sold inherently unreliable European brands was tolerated, whilst I drove an Aussie built car that got me to work on time most days.

It had been yet another singularly uneventful day at work the time the Maserati 105 disappeared, until my boss raised the alarm.

'Where's the bloody Maser Diablo?' he yelled across the yard intercom.

That was the first sign that something had gone seriously wrong. Under a bonnet my back straightened as if hit by lightning. I mean, it wasn't uncommon for customers to 'abandon' their pride and joy anywhere within the three acres of showroom and workshops that our dealership occupied; that the car had vanished after me, was.

When the next day the cops came around, I realised we had experienced a real earthquake. A car I had just serviced had gone missing, now the problem was tracking closer than I wanted.

'Where did you put it?' the stone-faced detective asked, checking his mobile as if for Lotto results.

'As I told my boss, out the side, there,' I pointed to the empty car bays, 'ready to be cleaned.'

'Why there?'

'We always put them there after servicing. Then the cleaner drives them around to the other side for the customer to pick them up later on.' A certain level of frustration crept into my voice.

'Don't leave town, we'll want to talk more later,' the skinny one replied. 'Anything else you want to tell us?'

Our car cleaner, Mikael, was seen as a 'cashie', someone my boss paid under the counter, an itinerant kid sent down to us in desperation from a job agency to clean the cars. We all thought he was a backpacker. Most likely on a gap year from somewhere in Europe. Certainly he was a diminutive but stocky guy who rarely went without a football cap or sunglasses, keeping himself to himself, even eating lunch in the corner of the wash bay. One time we passed side-on in the toilet doorway, me giving a customary greeting, 'How're they hanging?' He only grunted but limped off leaving behind a waft of what seemed to be cheap aftershave. Gay? I wondered. I certainly noticed he had a bad case of man boobs as we squeezed past one another. With sunglasses off he had the most wicked set of rimmed green eyes I'd yet seen. In just one look, stunning, abso-bloody-lutely, the eyes that is.

Whilst enthroned in the toilet cubicle, my head in my hands, a glint from the floor caught my eye. Reaching down, I saw it was a tubular remnant of cellophane wrapping from something I'd learnt from my sister that all women knew about each month but few men acknowledged. Hmm.

At least our dealership had an advantage over the others I'd worked in, it was the toilets. One time before, the boss' pregnant wife had been caught short and had to use the stinking staff dunny, complete with misaimed pools of urine and old phonebooks for paper. A month later, the builder and plumbers moved in, displacing all the old rotting floorboards, permanently stained porcelain bowls and cracked basins that dated back to when Noah was a lad. Yes, after the floodlit glass enclosed showroom, the glossy floor to ceiling tiled toilets were the centrepiece of our workplace, a place in which the boss had soon had the bottom foot cut off the cubicle doors to discourage time wasting.

And meeting place too. I only ran into Mikael there, his work-supplied white overalls several sizes too big for his frame, the cuffs rolled up, the only guy I knew to put the seat down and flush afterwards. Probably a bloody pansy. If only those iridescent green eyes of his hadn't enmeshed with mine I would have been happier. Soft-featured effeminate face too. Should I have been so attracted; maybe I was subconsciously gay? Not that I thought so.

Over several sessions the cops gave me a harder and harder time, especially as I was the last person to see the errant Maserati. They even dragged up my high school expulsion, my parents' divorce and a brief sojourn in juvenile detention. All the ghosts from a past supposedly pushed behind me out of sight. Because of all this, I nearly lost my job; it was only because of a spotless work history and mechanical prowess that I stayed. Just. And still under suspicion, a pariah in my own job, all the guys, my former workmates, suddenly became avid readers of motorcycle magazines whenever I was around. That hurt like nothing else.

A couple of weeks later I was out road testing a 911 Carrera after servicing, when the car parked on the left rang a distant doorbell in my mind, a white Porsche GT3. No spaces, so I pulled over, double parking, and ran back. By now I was sure it was one of ours and some fool had left the keys in the ignition, the full story yet to unfold. But as I reached in through the open window for the keys, a beat-up Nissan Patrol roared past and clipped my customer's double parked Carrera. Oh shit, and yet the 4WD barely hesitated, the swarthy passenger in the front seat angrily shaking his fist at me.

It was a long day arranging the panel beater, apologising to the customer and finally contacting the insurance company. To top it off, Mikael, the guy in the cleaning department had shot through, the queue of uncleaned cars mounted, so we all had to pitch in, hoses, sponges and water flying through the air. If it wasn't somewhat farcical, the scene of us guys coated in white foam could have been from a Scandinavian Christmas card.

Then the cops returned, my boss insisting on a fuller inquiry and upgrading all our security. Suddenly the place took on the appearance of a concentration camp with CCTV cameras on every corner. So within a few short days my name became 'shit', not a single guy would be seen in the same area as me. With the security tightened to near stranglehold, everyone suffered with the introduction of locked gates and a new key system; after all, few of our cars were worth less than $100K and a couple in the showroom over $500K. Even our labour rate was $200 an hour, not that we were paid an eighth of that into our bank accounts every fortnight, and in arrears too. And the police, after a couple of months they had diddly squat, but it was the 'squat' that set me thinking, not that it mattered in the end.

'Max, report to office, Max to the office.' The announcement came through the intercom.

No one got this without being sacked. Shit!

'You've been a very naughty boy, Max,' my boss said with a scowl, 'doing what you did. I'll have to let you go; you're no good for business.'

'But what about the cleaner?' I protested. It all seemed so unfair.

'Way too dumb, couldn't even speak English, his word against yours. Anyway, he's pissed off and can't be located.'

With a limp hand we shook and I left, not knowing exactly where I was heading.

But what was new?

And was my boss implicated? Or someone else in the workshop? Why didn't the police take it more seriously? Could it possibly be the car owners or their insurance companies involved? Who could I trust and which way did I turn?

At this stage I decided to recruit my young brother, a modern day gamer and computer geek. Owing me heaps and always on the cage for a few bucks, I sought repayment.

'Hey bro, I want to find someone.'

'Name?' was all he asked, his fingers poised over the keyboard.

I hesitated, then led with my best punch.

'First name, Mikael, no possibly Mikaela, surname Romano, aged 20 to 25, eastern European perhaps, probably on a 12 month work permit.'

Mark's eyebrows rose, 'That's it?'

'Not even sure about this much,' I said, 'though I could tell you when she had her last period.'

'Whoa, mate, way too much information. Leave it with me, I'll see what I can do.'

A week later I was summoned by text message. Like a schoolboy outside the principal's office I stood there.

'No Medicare, no Tax File Number, no address, came in 14 months ago from Budapest on a Hungarian passport so she is overstaying. That's it.'

'Bugger!'

Then Mark winked, 'But your clever brother does have a mobile number for you. Don't ask me how or tell anyone. Hacking is illegal.'

'My lips are sealed.'

'And if it clears my debt, we know where her last call was made from.'

'Done. Now where? When?'

'Port Nepean Road, Rosebud, around First Avenue. Yesterday afternoon.'

'We're looking for a car cleaner,' I said. 'My company deals in exclusive cars so attention to detail is essential.'

With the Employment Service slogan plastered on the wall, the wrinkled desk jockey could only say, 'I see.'

The good old Commonwealth Employment Service, right on the main road.

'Young, enthusiastic, short term, maybe longer, depends. May suit a backpacker.'

'Had one in this morning,' she said, her jowls quivering like a frill necked lizard, 'but no valid work permit. Now let's see,' she added, clicking through her computer screen. 'Ah yes, there's several young local fellows looking for a job. Shall I give you their details?'

As I strolled the shopping centres, then trawled down the main road, it reminded me of the old adage of looking for a needle in a haystack. So near and yet so far. But then, just as I pulled out to head home, there was something about the walk of the girl ahead. Slight limp too. Could be, no, yes, then she turned side on. With not much to go on, fate pulled like a beckoning finger. Sunglasses, short boyish hair, T-shirt and frayed denim shorts; I hit my mobile, she dived for her bag, so I pulled alongside. Bingo! Ah yes, her face and my fate. Gotcha!

I leant over and opened the door. 'Get in,' I said, 'or I'll call the police.'

Flipping her sunnies upwards, she hesitated, her emerald eyes flashing. 'Oh it is you,' she said, resignedly falling into the cracked vinyl seat. 'How did you find me?' her clipped voice was like biting into honeycomb.

'I know what you did, how you did it but not why,' I said.

Behind, an impatient horn barped so we moved off. Which way, did it matter; I wouldn't get my job back anyway.

'You would not understand,' she spoke so softly I could hardly hear, 'you want to screw me?'

'Is that all you think I want?'

'Do you always answer a question with a question?'

'Do you?' I said and we laughed, her smile lighting up her face and something deep down inside me stirred.

There was an indefinable charm about Mikaela, all indignation evaporated. OK, like a sweating stick of gelignite I was infinitely vulnerable but, then again, so was she.

As I drove along the highway, the backlit bay was in windless tranquillity beside us but my mind raced in overdrive.

'I've lost my job,' I said, glancing sideways, 'thanks to you.'

'I have no passport,' she said, 'they took it away with them.'

'And?'

'Maybe we need one another,' she said.

There's a headland at Dromana, 'Pope's Nose', the locals call it, where the waves crash in on northerlies, the green shallow waters shimmering over yellow sand amplifying the blue waves; it was there we stopped and watched the water. Blue, green and simply translucent. Minutes passed by quickly as the shimmering sunlit patterns in the water changed every second, how could anyone be bored with waves? Always changing, sometimes surprising, never ending, much like life itself. Gradually, I became aware of a closer presence, her head resting on my shoulder. There we sat, our lost souls merging from what had happened but now more in the present. Without even thinking I leant over ever so tentatively and kissed her head, about where her fine hair parted. Would she notice or mind? Was it my imagination when she relaxed even lower against my spindly frame? Then, when I glanced down, her fingers were inside my palm, her fingers lay curled like petals of a rose. As we watched in the gloom, a higher being turned down the sun, the city lights sparkled on the horizon far away in answer. An earthly reality would soon assert itself.

'Mikaela,' I started.

'You are different,' she said, 'to what I thought.'

'You've got to go to the police, tell them what you know.'

'I am scared,' she stopped, touching my cheek with a hand that trembled and added, 'Max.' It was then I knew we had a chance. Slim but what else?

'Mikaela, I don't have much to offer you.'

'It is enough.'

Like in the toilets some months before, our eyes meshed and I was lost to a soul I'd sought all my life. This time our lips found one another's and our fates, whatever they turned out to be, were sealed.

In all I only served six months from a year reduced on good behaviour, but would I be met at the gates by someone with mesmerising eyes of which I would never tire?

'Mikaela!'

Suddenly she lurched forward as if tripping, the two soft plops barely audible. In her eyes I saw bewilderment with red roses bursting from her blouse. Then my chest pounded likewise and, like punctured balloons, we collided and fell. Our fingertips touched, our wedding rings clicked, then blackness descended and I felt no more. Others may have heard the 4WD leaving but not us, not ever.

Death is not what it seems.

What about Emily's Father?

When a small curly headed figure, about four or thereabouts, slowly walked past, peering in, naturally I waved. Then she went past from the other direction, then back again, almost like she was playing a game of hide and seek. My curiosity was instantly aroused, how could I help but smile back? She looked kind of familiar, something, as I shook my head in disbelief, I knew wasn't really possible.

'Are you looking for something or someone?' I asked, opening the door.

'Is this where the pictures are?' she answered.

'Oh, that was a while ago, young lady,' I said, squatting down and looking at her more closely. 'Do I know your name?'

Then my breath faltered. Here was the girl I had gone to kindergarten with 24 years before. Brunette, pert nose and inquisitive eyes, but now definitely her mother's daughter.

Shaking her head, bright eyes gazed intently into mine. 'My name is Emily,' she said with an emphatic upturned nose. 'What's yours?'

'Thomas. But I can show you where your mummy watched them. Would you like to come in?' I stood, flipping over the door sign to 'Closed'.

The look of wonderment on Linda's daughter's face spread as we trooped hand-in-hand past my accountancy office that was built into the foyer. Though dimly lit with few of the globes in the shell-shaped lights glowing, the old Lyrics Theatre still retained a certain magic with the art deco plaster reliefs on wall and ceiling, the fake plaster columns towering overhead her diminutive size. In front, the rows of maroon cracked leather seats must have appeared as a mountain range to her, the old curtain hanging lopsided.

I pointed up to the glass windows at the back, 'And the pictures came down from there and showed up on the screen behind the curtain here.'

'Where did Mummy sit?'

'Just here,' I said, 'seat B2, and I sat next to her in B1.'

My hand flew up, remembering my slapped cheek as if it was yesterday.

'Are you my daddy?'

'No, sweetie, I'm not your daddy. Your mummy and I were just friends.' Then I took a risk, 'I have a surprise for you, young lady, a special surprise.'

Her eyes widened.

'But it's not a lolly or an ice-cream, Emily. I'd like you to meet a friend of mine and your mummy's. He lives down here in the theatre. His name is Bugs Bunny. Would you like to meet him?'

As I thought, my visitor was unable to curb her natural inquisitiveness. Somehow I'd almost forgotten about the innocence of children, a priceless time of life when fun and pleasure can be achieved through sheer simplicity, the joy infectious to all but the most hardened of hearts. Everyone and everything is trusted then. Distrust, hate, shame and guilt are learnt later.

Sitting her in B2, I raced up the stairs and hit multiple switches. The film easily loaded, soon ready to roll. For a moment I thought she'd leave in the gloom but then the curtains opened, if a little jerkily, and Bugs appeared. 'Eh, what's up Doc?' he agelessly greeted us with his nasal voice.

Sitting alongside Emily, seeing her enraptured for every second of the whole seven minutes made all the effort worthwhile; another time the darkness hid unresolved damp eyes. It was then I realised my life had more ends than knots, frayed ends that needed to be tied up.

Back in my office, over a glass of milk, we were discussing the vagaries of raising rabbits in a rural town when a tall shadow went past the front window. Issues about mixamatosis and callicivirus evaporated. Ah, Emily's mother and bearing an anxious expression too. From the start I knew I was courting trouble, was my other cheek now going to sting? Turning, she saw us and stormed in. Maybe it was the sheer angst, but Linda was simply breathtaking, I hadn't realised what time could wreak. But inside me, nothing had changed. If anything, my feelings had only deepened.

'Emily?' she said, initialling ignoring my presence. 'What are you doing here?'

'I've met a friend of Thomas,' her daughter said proudly.

Linda's eyebrows rose in question.

'Oh yes and what's his name?'

'Bugs Bunny. He's a rabbit, a naughty one. He takes carrots from, from, from ...'

'Elmer Fudd,' Linda and I spoke in unison.

'Yes, Elmer Fudd. Isn't that a funny name, Mummy? He's a farmer and grows carrots. Now if I had a rabbit ...'

Linda interrupted the prattle that promised to continue way longer than the film's seven minutes. 'We'd better be getting home. Grandma will be getting worried, come along Emily,' she said before turning to me, her eyes blazing, 'You and I need to talk.'

Behind her, the distraught look on Emily's face was thought-provoking, as if she could do little to appease her mother.

'I'll put that in my diary, shall I?' I said to no one in particular as they filed past the window. Then Emily's grinning face came back around the corner and she waved before being dragged away.

I'd heard we had a new teacher on transfer at the primary school, so added to Linda's mother being unwell, and now my recent visitor, suddenly everything made sense, well, nearly everything.

Strangely, as an only child I wasn't ever lonely. No, I was the most popular kid at school with everyone trying to be my best friend, especially on Fridays before the latest picture hit town on Saturday. In the schoolyard they would gather round. 'Sit here, Thomas, next to me. Would you like one of my mother's cakes, Thomas? Oh Thomas, I do like your hair,' the girls fawned, while with the boys it was, 'You're battin' first, Tommy,' or 'Fancy bowlin' this week, mate,' or, 'Eh Thommo, we're goin' yabbyin' down the river Sunday arvo, wanna come?'

Moving into my teens my status escalated to almost god-like, the girls even more blatant, my mates clustered around me as ants surround a picnic table seeking a choice crumb.

'I've heard it's a good one, Thomas. Ali McGraw is so cute, don't you think?' or 'Clint Eastward is the best, kapow,' they exclaimed, practising their draw with index finger and thumb outstretched.

Ah yes, I was the projectionist's son, the gangly guy who had free access to the local picture theatre. The one who could take whom he pleased, 'Just one each week though, son, alright? Don't abuse it, every penny counts,' Dad said.

My male mates dwindled as I exploited my 'Pass' with only girls. With storm-like hormones raging I could have that week's prettiest girl sitting alongside; rarely did they mind my arm behind their shoulders or lower down at the front either. By 15 I saw myself as the unassailable 'breast-stroke champion' of our town, despite there being no swimming pool within miles! Located out in the farming, orchard and dairy district about two hours drive north of Melbourne, Shepparton's cluster of houses and district farms had only a few thousand souls, but the pictures became nightly events as Dad struggled to meet the mortgage repayments on the 1930's theatre. Fortunately, the Saturday matinees were an institution. Once, I overheard someone saying that my dad would show a film to a sleeping dog if he only had the threepence. They were right too.

The 35 millimetre films came in large tin reinforced wooden boxes, hexagonally shaped and so heavy Dad had a trolley on which we'd stack the unwieldy reels. Then from the train station, where they'd arrive once a week on the Vic-Rail goods train, he'd slowly wheel the trolley all the way along the main street to the theatre, me trailing and loaded to eyelevel with the accompanying posters to be glued up around town.

Up in the bio-box it was another world. Accessible via the narrowest, steepest stairway meant the film boxes had to be manhandled. When Dad hefted them, he grew red in the face and wheezed for ages afterwards. When I was younger, at primary school, we'd actually hoick them together, one on each side, step by laborious step, but later carrying them myself as my shoulders broadened. At the top of the steps two huge monsters with gigantic disc-like eyes stood, the lenses pointing out as cannons towards the tiny glass windows. Down in the gloom below I could faintly make out the maroon velvet stage curtains in front of row after row of flip-down seats some said were harder than a bag of wheat. Often I heard Dad mutter under his breath, 'Did they come for the show or a bloody lounge chair?'

Lit with an incredible electric arc, the film projector's light had automatic feed but sometimes the carbon rods would burn too fiercely, the scene down below getting more bleached by the minute as a cloudless summer day before suddenly turning jet black when the rod disintegrated. Other times the arc light would dim, the picture prematurely going into a nightfall effect. Both times Dad would be woken from his slumber by the whistles, catcalls or the thunder of stamping feet on the red gum floorboards, the dust rising in the theatre as a spring ground mist in the surrounding paddocks. On the theatre's back wall there was a bell push for Bill, the pensioner-usher, to warn Dad upstairs, but all three were temperamental.

Perched up in the bio-box Dad relished his role of teaching me how to load, thread the film and rewind the reels along with all the other procedure. No football field or cricket pitch, this was our twilight world we shared as equals. Even under Dad's tutelage I found all the lights, curtain switches and the advertisements for the local funeral service daunting, but most times I had someone waiting for me downstairs, someone whose teenage breasts irresistibly tempted my searching fingers, my goal to sample every eligible girl, not the easiest task with tricky buttons, press studs or zips. Then there was their bra to navigate around. Strangely few seemed to mind my wanderings in the anonymous dark, especially when they were eating free popcorn and engrossed in a film

I'd seen many times before. Never went any further though, too scared I guess.

There was, however, a girl I especially wanted to get closer to. Tall, slim and hazel-eyed daughter of the State Savings Bank manager, Linda Mulligan was the only like-aged girl who avoided going to the pictures; indeed she seemed to watch from a distance with a certain disdain as her friends flirted unashamedly. If only she knew the haughty poking out of her tongue formed an irresistible challenge. Ah, Linda, the only classmate who had not yielded to my charm and been expertly assessed. This, her compelling eyes and something else I couldn't quite put my finger on appealed to me.

Finally, when 'Anne of Green Gables' came on, I determined to make my move. It was a hit, how could she resist? Every girl in the entire school wanted to go with me, but I chose Linda. It was now or never.

'Hey Linda,' I said nonchalantly, swaggering as only a 16-year-old can after watching a diet of American films, 'Watcha doing Sat'day night? It's Anne of Green Gables, wanna come?'

For what seemed several minutes, she hesitated and I could see her thinking furiously. It was a time when author Lucy Montgomery, creator of effervescent red-haired Anne, appealed to us teenagers as no other.

'We are meant to be studying, exams are in a week, Thomas,' Linda remonstrated before yielding to the inevitable, 'but I 'spose I could, if my parents agree,' she added as a rider. 'And you'll have to keep your hands to yourself.'

In answer I raised my hands in surrender, but not in innocence.

'I'll pick you up at seven, Lindy.'

'No,' she pouted her as yet un-kissed lips, 'I'll meet you there and it's straight home afterwards. By the way, it's Linda, as you well know.'

Before she sat down that memorable night I managed to get my arm across the back of her seat so rested my hand on her bare shoulder even before intermission. Inwardly, I congratulated myself on a promising first half with still more to follow. Dad's 'Intermission' was always an unscheduled break between reels where he gave everyone a chance to buy Mum's handmade Choctops or more popcorn from the tiny kiosk in the foyer, the oldies with dodgy bladders to visit the toilet and my mates to go around the side for a furtive smoke.

After intermission the film really hotted up and so I began to make my practised moves. Light finger stroking on the shoulders, a seemingly accidental brush across her blouse, top button gently teased undone ... oh yes, but then my hand was firmly gripped and placed back on my knee. Alright, but one not to give up, while Linda sighed over the unrequited love on the screen, I persisted with even more subtle moves, getting fingertips inside her blouse and surreptitiously edging down past lace to her soft breast. Could I make it to the nipple by the last reel, I wondered. Oh boy.

Suddenly my cheek was on fire, the loudest slap coinciding with the quietest scene and echoing like a 303 rifle shot. Ironically, it was the scene where Gilbert Blythe was having the same degree of luck with Anne. Like a startled jackrabbit Linda jumped up, her figure clearly outlined on the screen and stormed out. To avoid a hundred stares I slunk down in the seat, my reputation and confidence in tatters.

I changed tack.

'Mr Donaldson says we need study partners if we're contemplating uni, Linda. What do you think?' I asked.

Her eyes rose to the ceiling before sweeping over me somewhat scathingly, like I was Jack the Ripper. Amongst the class it was common knowledge she would have preferred Adrian Forsyth, the brightest kid in our year by far. I sensed she was getting frustrated waiting for him to ask, something that wouldn't be happening since he'd been bribed silent with a year's free entry to the theatre.

'I guess so,' she said with a measured reluctance, 'as long as that's all you've got on your mind.'

'Maybe we can discuss the details on the way home after school.'

Linda leaned forward, her voice taking on a most dangerous note, 'And if you ever touch me again, you'll live to regret it. Understand?'

This time I raised my hands in supplication. Inside however, my heart beat a little faster.

That year in the first term I surrendered my usual pursuits of the flesh at the theatre and for once applied myself to study. It hadn't escaped my attention that this was a once in a lifetime opportunity and the sacrifice that it required of my parents; everything they had was invested in the theatre. Then, to my own bewilderment and that of the teachers, my term marks rose meteorically; I found myself enjoying the intellectual challenge, now I was contemplating university as a serious option, especially with Linda and me firing off one another as ricocheting bullets. How else could I get her attention? Not only that but the field of finance appealed, an area where I could help people manage their money and maybe earn a good living, unlike that of my ageing father.

When the picture first dimmed, I thought little of it. Strangely, the bell push made no difference; I could faintly hear it ringing up in the bio-box. Come on Dad, I implored. Finally, with only the soundtrack filling the blackened theatre, I took the stairs two at a time and pushed open the door against an unexpected resistance, a black half-polished shoe in view. This sight was my first experience with death; my father slumped lifeless on his wooden stool, his legs splayed out. He would show no more films, his ailing heart had burst, his pulse gone forever. Ah, poor Dad.

Unlike him, the film sprang to life with my quick twist of the arc feed knob, the thunder of stamping feet stopped, but life was never to be the same again.

Like a good son born after the war, I held my composure with straight back, my mother's teachings that only Italians cry at funerals foremost in my mind. Then as the sun went down and as my mother and I cleared the wake table, a tall figure filled the back door. It was Linda, my study mate; she had foreseen the inevitable ramifications of Dad's death.

'Can I see you for a minute?' she said, flicking her head to outside, her voice subdued.

'I'm sorry about your father, Thomas,' she started.

But then my shallowly buried emotions burst to the surface, my lips felt tears when she kissed me. It was the sweetest kiss of compassion and went straight to an ailing heart. If there was a definable moment Linda filled my being, it was then.

'I'll be thinking of you,' she said and disappeared.

At the same time the town gained their youngest ever theatre operator. Linda continued on that year at school without me, even beating Adrian Forsyth for dux. Then university took her from sight.

But now she was back. Warily, Linda and I faced one another like cornered boxers within ropes, neither conceding the first words.

'What about Emily's father?' I said.

For a long moment she hesitated, 'Seeing you asked, well, one night going home from uni I was raped. That's it.'

My eyes watered. Yet suddenly the picture became clearer, as when focussing the projector lens on the blurry image far away on the screen. It explained Emily's life, that of a barely wanted child, a constant reminder of something not freely given but taken by force. And the lack of a father's reconciling love.

I reached for her hand; this time our fingers meshed.

Eileen's Story

Most likely Eileen, not our grandmother, was the real matriarch of our close-knit family with our grandparents living just twenty yards away. Somewhat aptly named, we wondered if one leg of Eileen's wasn't somewhat shorter than the other. And if Eileen had a weakness, it must have been in her spindly legs. Maybe the years had rocked her world mercilessly, but eccentric Grandma would have none of it. No, Eileen was part of the family, on her side, she emphasized with a defiant toss of her grey-haired head, and entitled to attend all gatherings whether we liked it or not. And so, as usual without words, Eileen had spoken.

Stiff backed and sparsely framed, her ample bottom padded with what appeared to be shabby upholstery fabric, Eileen presided in vice-regal fashion at head of table over our family gatherings. Her golden eyes, more like tarnished drawing pins, reflected the dusty chandelier's dim light overhead and would appear to follow us around no matter which way we turned. These were times when every chair was pressed into service as we three kids, accompanied by parents, trooped across the street for a Sunday meal with Grandma and Grandpa. A time when best behaviour was expected. Whilst Mum frowned on bad language from us, strangely Dad could say 'bloody.' This was post-war Melbourne when children were to be seen but not always heard unless something polite and interesting was to be said. With older female siblings, how hard was that for a young brother to get a word in edgewise! We were expected to sit up, eat up and shut up.

Not that we were game to say a word, Eileen also had the most appalling manners, with a single movement of her wonky leg sending anyone she took an aversion to slithering to the floor. With short, rounded feet pivoting like castors she would screech should anyone try to push her around where she didn't want to go; her gait was more of a half-glide, swivel and step; she would move in her own sweet time. And direction too, even if the gentlest of hands went around her softly curved back.

To sit on Eileen's wide lap was considered a great honour; a rare event when sitting down became an exhilarating experience. In a second you could sway like a drunkard one way, the next you were hanging on to her sides for grim death. However, if one sat up, back straight, hardly daring to move a muscle, Eileen was happy. But try to kick a sister back under the table and suddenly the floor rose up to hit your head. Such a wicked unpredictable temper Eileen had in dispensing family justice. It was as though she lacked the binding glue of life in her own personal existence and took frustration out on all around.

My father, an only son, often tried to put Eileen to rights with articulate hand gestures and subtle squeezes. Somehow he sensed his mother's pet relation was embarrassing to others. Should someone attempt to argue, Eileen would bide her time then let loose, no way would she broke any criticism sitting down.

Finally, after one confrontation too many, when she let Dad down unexpectedly, we stifled laughter as he contemplated life looking up at the ornate plaster ceiling rose lying on his back. With pursed lips he took Eileen aside and bodily carried her across the road home, for once not heeding anyone's concern. We watched her legs hanging limply from his arms and exchanged meaningful glances.

When, sometime later, Dad let Eileen out of his workshop, her behaviour had changed forever. It was as though the break in relations had mended her errant ways, she would let no more people down. With wooden expression and stiff legged from sitting alone in the dark, she was relegated to the corner on trial, but soon necessity prevailed.

Despite grandparents and now parents passing on, Eileen has survived another 60 years, even a proposed tongue-in-cheek name change to Noelene didn't stick, unlike the space-age adhesive that now held her joints firmly together.

Bearing no human frailty, they built Edwardian chairs to last.

Caution: Duel Control

Finding my most intimate rubbish strewn, bomb-like, across the road initiated my battle with the stray neighbourhood dog. Bin over again! That it escalated to a feud with the council worker was not consciously of my doing, no way.

Rubbish rage? Heinz started it.

Seeking a unique all Aussie female identity these days isn't easy; just try erasing embarrassing university Facebook photos, but you get the idea, OK? As for exclusivity, I wasn't going to let myself be emotionally manipulated by some boozed, groping Neanderthal from the dinosaur age. Definitely no denigrating role of marriage and childbearing for me thank you, just because males have one more rib. Supposedly.

Any relationship should be based on honesty, equality and mutual respect: I sought Internet advice.

Open mouth, cavernous in wonder, my choice sat there stunned on our first date.

'This is how I see it, Trent,' I stated.

Deep, captivating brown eyes and retreating hairline made him seem a lot older than me, though he had claimed to be similar in years. He was totally cute though, while his long, strong hands said heaps.

'The computer says we're 99% compatible but, just to be sure, I've put all the household duties in a hat. We'll let chance determine who does what. Absolutely no one is telling me what I'm doing in my life.'

And that's how he got house cleaning duties and I got to put out the bin. Fate had also decreed that he put down the toilet lid and clean up his own drips. Perfect. But that I had to drag the voluminous bin up the driveway in the dark, well that made it nearly perfect.

The computer matching site had Trent listed as my ideal e-life partner, a high level professional involving twin, alternating responsibilities. Apparently, he held an executive environmental recycling position as well as being on a steering committee, but one always leaving well before my frantic later departure. It's not that I'm disorganised. As if! But mornings were never my best time of day especially with a rushed breakfast. More of an evening person, I swoon over soft candlelit dinners as Trent has discovered. Coming along nicely, his cooking had improved thanks to those TV programs and our flat was tidy and spotless. Generally. Once he got the hang of emptying the vacuum cleaner I had high hopes of elevating his position and status in the commitment stakes. But could I trust him? We were only up to page four in the Kama Sutra due to Trent's sore back. Trent promised to seek some physio but unfortunately neither of us is double jointed, or maybe we've just got the book upside down. If only he wouldn't drool when reading; once I caught him kissing my neck and poking his tongue into my ear. What page was that again? Strangely pleasant though.

My rubbish rage escalated when the truck deliberately refused to wait for my bin. Bugger! Customer focus, the council manifesto stated, well hello! In fact, I'm sure he sped up past our place and collected everyone else's just to spite me. I stood there dumbfounded. Was my rubbish not good enough? Why was he rushing so? 'Caution: Dual Control' said the sticker on the back. That'd be right, typical male, like both sides were useless, the sticker should have been spelt 'duel'. Bring it on, I thought.

The following week the bin was overflowing; the stench wafting under our bedroom window rank enough to make any sort of lovemaking position untenable. Nor could the local dog ignore this bin's feast. OK, I admit surreptitiously putting much waste food inside, my appetite had diminished lately along with Trent's greasy cooking. Should I mention more salads and vegetables?

But in the midst of getting ready for work, I again felt uneasy. As the shower water cascaded down, I thought hard. What was it? But then suddenly it came to me as if I'd been struck by a lightning bolt. Surely not that time of the month, no, much worse.

Rubbish day! The bin! Oh shit!

A tad off my usual last minute, split-second timing, I ran after the truck, dragging the recalcitrant bin behind. Yet every bloody time I drew near, the hydraulic Michelin arm would shoot out, the bin arcing up into the cavernous mouth, then carelessly flung aside. Just when I could nearly touch the truck he'd pull off. Deliberate evasion, I thought. Prick! Just wait until I caught up, then he'd get some dialogue. Now panting, could I put in one more Olympic sprint and catch up? But what drug-free, overweight and unfit athlete had to drag a putrid 240 litre wheelie bin behind them?

Pretty soon I became exhausted. At the last house, just as I drew alongside, no one could wear a more determined grimace, the truck pivoted around the corner on two wheels as if a Formula One racer and sped off down the court. Oh no!

Breathless I stood there alone and defeated, but not without an awestruck audience. Up and down the street people were lined up, supposedly to put their bins back, a somewhat awed look on their faces. It was then I realised my trailing dressing-gown had slipped open, revealing a distinct lack of underwear and exposing more than was polite. I had thought the sea breeze seemed all too fresh around my nether regions. Whoops!

But first to regain my dignity; I shook a clenched fist at the departing truck and tightened the cord around my waist. Head held high, spirit unbroken, I sauntered undaunted past Alonso, the leering, asthmatic pensioner with gap-ridden teeth, smiled at Mrs Forsyth, an Alzheimer's pensioner, waved to Harry, the king of compo next door and returned from where I'd started my bin marathon. Apart from complete loss of breath and dignity, just what had I achieved?

Revenge is a bin left unemptied.

Always fiercely independent, I decided to declare war on the roaming neighbourhood mongrel that pushed bins left out overnight over as if they were skittles in a bowling alley. Not for nothing was I a builder's daughter of great repute who could show the world of what she was made. The thought of enlisting Trent was never on my mind; he had his duties and I had mine.

That weekend, the neighbourhood air screeched with sounds of concrete dyna-bolts securing a certain bin onto the driveway. No one could doubt its stature. Trent, obviously still preoccupied over page five, bless him, seemed lost with diagnosing the vacuum cleaner's loss of suction. Should I enlighten him that this coincided with the loss of my best French knickers? No, probably not.

'No Marie, this is child's play. You can do it, watch and learn,' I repeated to myself with barred teeth.

Why was nothing happening, oh yes, the power point switch was off. Why wasn't the drill drilling; shouldn't it be going the other way? I wondered. 'Typical Chinese crap,' I answered myself out loud, 'designed for use in the Northern Hemisphere,' before quickly switching the drill to clockwise.

Much noise, dust and vibration later, causing all and sundry to peer past their kitchen curtains, the bin was now firmly bolted down against dog attack. I could leave it out at night and relax in the morning at last. Yes! No male, not even a cunning canine one, would better me.

Of course this was the day the truck arrived late; I'd left for work, the bin standing triumphant on the driveway like the Eiffel Tower.

However, it was upon my return that night, when the flashing lights reflected in the gloom made me wonder. Ambulance? Had old Alonso next door finally run out of life's oxygen? But then that didn't explain the fire brigade. Had Mrs Forsyth put her electric kettle on the gas range yet again? As I drew closer nothing really explained the myriad of emergency vehicles clustered around the driveway, especially the hazardous chemicals response team, the tow truck, council ute and police car.

Trent was evidently home from work early too, wringing his hands seemingly quite concerned about the rubbish truck lying on its side. Serve the driver right, I thought, must have sharply avoided my bin once too often. Then it hit me. Oh no. What had I done?

He grabbed me on the way down just as the sky suddenly began to whirl. A dark nightfall came early and I was lost.

As if in a dream, I came to, how much later who could say? The uniformed paramedic quickly gave me the all-clear.

'You're fine, everything's OK,' before adding with a knowing smile, 'considering your condition.'

Darkness descended again. This time Trent's concerned face lent over me, grabbing my hand. Instantly I felt reassured. What an absolute sweetie, how could I possibly doubt him? Alright, I loved him. Hang on, what did she say, considering my condition? What condition?

'Marie love, don't worry about a thing, once they get it back on its wheels, my truck is most likely undamaged.'

'Your truck?'

When Dad
Kicked the Bucket

Melbourne, 1958

For those who'd met our Dad, it was always memorable experience, but probably something his students strove to forget, like their daily homework. Tall as a leaning goal post on the school oval with penetrating school teacher eyes that missed little, he was typical of ex-servicemen who had experienced World War II. Yes, we kids were baby boomers and I wonder if Mum and Dad weren't trying to make up for lost time from their Sunday morning sleep-ins with closed bedroom door. OK, too much information I hear you saying. I agree.

These days it's hard to describe or even imagine a world without mobile phones, TV and reliable electricity. Internet, what was that? Even the idea was inconceivable in our wildest dreams. Nor did Mum work, not in a paid sense anyhow, although she braved icy floors to light the stove before Dad stirred and ironed after we were meant to be in bed. Women's Liberation, was that the brand of those new fangled female thingies?

The arrival of TV in '56, only black and white of course, just in time for the Olympics, was a time of great excitement. However the anticipation of getting an Aussie-made set in our household was somewhat dulled, like the screen, by several years of plaintive pleading. Our TV diet had to be satiated by shivering outside the nearby Walton's store window or arranging to 'visit' friends at crucial show times.

Black outs, now politically cleansed into 'power outages', were the norm. We weren't known as baby boomers for nothing, what else did our parents have to do in the darkness but replenish a generation stolen by an overseas war? The tattered cardboard boxes of Monopoly, Chinese Checkers, Snakes and Ladders grew dusty while my futile efforts at Charades were forgotten. Hopefully.

Once the homework was done, our nightly 'theatre' consisted of three distinct rows, Mum and Dad having the good 'Fler' lounge chairs, the occupants of the front stalls sprawled at their feet in front of the open fire. These stalls came with the onerous duties of stoking the flames and watching out for errant sparks known to leave a large brown spot on the rug accompanied by pungent smell, not unlike my noxious brother. For us older ones, the rear couch suffered poor TV visibility and warmth, however compensated by a little less parental supervision. Of course, everyone was forbidden to move unnecessarily in case it disrupted the reception from the 'Rabbit's ears' antenna perilously positioned on top of our state-of-the-art 24 inch AWA Radiola set. That the set was made locally in Melbourne proved handy when new valves were needed to freeze the flickering horizontal or vertical hold. The reliability of modern electronics, like the local TV serviceman, had yet to arrive.

Already our bedrooms were strictly out-of-bounds to boys and even with 'approved' visits, the door had to remain resolutely open, Mum usually hovering close by. Her best tactic was to uncharacteristically Hoover the hall carpets whilst we attempted to conjugate French verbs. Few overstayed their welcome, 'Mais j'ai une idée,' my classmate, and father of our children 10 years later, said. 'Quel?' I breathed back into his ear, our hands holding as if the future depended on it.

On blackouts, our family worked as a well-oiled unit, unlike the Yallourn power station down in the Latrobe Valley. On the mantelpiece stood the torch, filled with new Eveready batteries that would lead the designated person to the kitchen cupboard where a stash of candles and boxes of Bryant and May matches lay. Everyone else sat motionless. What else did one do in the darkness?

This particular summer's evening, things went a little awry, although I suspected my little brother of some midnight under-the-blanket reading of Australian Post, the bikini cover girl requiring exhaustive perusal. Flat batteries. This meant much bumping of shins and vague mutterings whilst finally, after what seemed a lifetime, a ghost-like, candle-lit figure bumped from side to side down the draughty hallway. This journey appeared to require much time and bad language, punctuated by Mum's protestations.

But, in retrospect, it must have been my sister's tripping on the rug and spilling of molten wax on a bare stomach that unleashed that night's fury. In an instant Dad rose as a rocket on cracker night and hopped around like a Highland dancer on heat just as the next door's dog sometimes did. In frustration Dad's legs lashed out, one foot kicking the wood bucket normally empty due to my illustrious brother's tardiness to perform chores. This time, however, his term report had progressed further down the alphabet. This meant the bin was heavily stacked in order to keep parental criticism to a minimum. Much like his maths score. These were the days when the parents took the teacher's side and gave as good again in the privacy of home. With Dad's ingrown toenail now fiery, he managed to stand on a hot coal dislodged from the fire. If only he had a firewalker's faith and gone to church on Sundays as we had to, it wouldn't have hurt, I wondered.

However, offended at having his tail stood on, Toddles, our family cat, resenting changes to the seating situation, promptly sank his razor sharp teeth into the offending item, Dad's other big toe.

That's when the lights came on, the TV crackled into life and the position of my study mate's hand down my school blouse was suddenly revealed by a glaring overhead 100 watt light. 'Vous sein est magnifigue,' had just been hotly whispered into my ear. 'T'pense?' I had replied with a tremble, 'd'plus a la droit, s'il vous plaît.'

'Oh shit!' Dad yelled at a volume as if he was calling his school to assembly. Even the antenna quivered. 'Merde,' Trent and I dutifully translated.

'How many times have I told you, Roy, no bad language in front of the children,' Mum admonished. 'Oh look, In Melbourne Tonight's just begun,' she said, leaning down and squinting between his hairy legs at the screen. 'Pity it's so small, stand aside will you love, you're not made of bloody glass. Ah, it's Graham Kennedy, now's that's another good laugh.'

A Fair Deal

Melbourne, 2015

I thought I knew everything there was to be known about my father. No secrets, he'd always said. Dad and me versus the world.

'Someone left a message for you today, Dad,' I said, 'but they'll ring back.'

Immersed in my spag bol he grunted. My turn for cooking that night after school, so his turn to wash up. A good deal in my 16 year old view, seemed few kids had the full complement of two parents or four grandparents anyway. At least Dad's mum was cool, always on her iPad and computer. My refuge, the granny flat out the back. Best of all, if I did well in Year 11, Dad said he'd start teaching me to drive. Deal.

But then, like climbing a sand dune, my world slipped, ever so slightly at first.

'Hello. Yes, this is Bernard Cafferty. Who? Cara, what! You're here? And after all this long too.' He paused, 'Alright, I'll get back to you.'

'Who was that, Dad?' I said, never seeing such alarm before. If the conversation was weird, his shocked look was worse. Body stiff as a board, it appeared like he had stopped breathing.

'Dad? Dad, answer me. Who was that?'

'Just someone I used to know,' he said, now standing at the sink, white fingers clenched. 'Haven't you got homework or something, Piers?'

Using last number redial didn't take a doctorate the next night. Not usually driven by snooping, OK, so my Dad had an occasional girlfriend whose moaning lulled me asleep with muffled giggling, but this was different. School and footy training kept me busy, while work occupied most of his hours. No secrets.

'Hello, I believe you rang my dad Bernie Cafferty last night. He seemed upset and I was wondering if everything was alright.'

Silence. 'Hello?'

'Who is this?'

'Piers Cafferty.'

'Hmm, suppose I shouldn't have rung. It was long ago. Your mum mightn't approve anyway.'

'I don't have a mum; she died when I was little. It's just Dad and me.'

'No,' the voice hesitated, 'let's leave it. Goodbye.'

If my thoughts weren't already overloaded by apprehension, suspicion took over. No secrets.

Waiting until Saturday night was only just achievable. We'd won by four goals, he'd cancelled Katy and a bottle of wine was half dead on the kitchen bench.

'Dad, who was Cara?'

Again that look of shock. Bullseye.

'Cara, I don't know any Cara.'

'She rang last night. You've never mentioned her before. I would have remembered.'

A long sigh erupted as though his last breath.

'Oh Piers, now is as good a time as any, I guess,' he said, as if a lifetime battle lost.

We'd had the 'birds and bees' chat several years before. But I knew Dad had travelled in his early twenties, mainly around Europe with several others. After a beer his eyes would light up describing silly escapades. I knew them all, my favourites his souveniring Oktoberfest beer steins and yanking down paralytic bus mates knickers so they could piddle and be sick into a bucket simultaneously. Didn't take too much imagination to fill in the spaces; girls, grog, and games. Aussie rite of passage. Indeed, I idly wondered if this wasn't an option after Year 12, retracing Dad's footsteps across the world.

'You see, Piers, all those years ago, there was this one person though, who really got under my skin. She was 20, a little younger than me, out to see the world,' he said. 'We were meant to be travel partners, two in a wheezing rusted-out Kombi, no complications, but somehow ...'

'Dad, you can tell me. Sounds like you fell for her.'

'Big time, son. The full catastrophe. First love and all that. Inside I would love her forever, but then things got complicated, really complicated.'

Dad's eyes glistened just like when Grandpa died. I pursed my lips. How could love be complicated? Admittedly classmate Kirsten had looked at me askance when a movie was first suggested but Facebook rumour suggested she was really keen but loath to admit. Maybe I could convert a smile into something more.

'She fell pregnant. At first I wasn't sure it was mine. She'd known another guy before me, but no, it was ours.'

'What happened then?'

'Cara organised an abortion, quite legal in UK even then.'

'So you got rid of a brother or sister I had.'

'No, Piers, we didn't. With her stomach bulging by the day somehow I convinced her to go the distance and give birth but her condition was for the baby to be given up for adoption. That was the deal. She wasn't ready for parenthood; still wanted to work and travel more. Wasn't ready to settle down or even sure I was the one for her.'

'So I have brother or sister out there?'

'Let me finish. This is not easy, OK? Some might have been content with that deal and moved on. But I just couldn't, I swore I'd always love a child of mine,' Dad looked out the window as if reading a smudgy script smeared by fingers on the fogged-up glass.

'There was this Polish girl in the backpacker's hostel, Louisa. Nice kid. Wanted to move to Australia. We brokered a deal; we'd get married, I'd adopt and keep him, she'd get residency. It seemed a fair deal, but one Cara never knew about though.'

'All these years you never said a single word about being married before Mum, or even me having a half brother,' I said. So much for no secrets, I thought, and if you couldn't trust your dad who could you trust?

Dad's slumped shoulders shrugged. 'We divorced. It was only a sham marriage so she could live here. Don't know even where she is now. And if I've misled you, this I regret.'

'And Cara?'

At that Dad pulled me towards him, his all encompassing arms stifling most doubts about love.

'Son, Cara is your mother.'

To Coin a Phrase

'Well?' asked Grandma.

'What's the currency of the situation, Dad?' my father added from behind his hand.

Suddenly everyone paused, and, for a moment, time and breathing stopped. Six pairs of eyes scanned Grandpa's face for hope. Was surgery his last resort?

You see Christmas at 4 Devon Street, Croydon, was always a time of great emotion. Anticipation, excitement and barely restrained commotion accompanied by the inevitable sibling rivalry. Subtle, as if! Shins were kicked, ribs prodded and tongues poked out, we three kids did it all. The riddle as to why I was saddled with two older sisters, but no supporting brother, Mum never deigned to solve. Hmm. At least we had grandparents living opposite us, a handy refuge in times of extreme family crisis; a missing fly button to be sewn, last minute cup of sugar or questionless hug.

It appeared our Christmas was modelled on a strange tradition, a hot roast meal in the middle of the day surpassing even our sun-crunchy school sandwiches, all while during boiling summers. Why had not our Anglo-Saxon forebears corrected menus for the southern hemisphere seasons we have to wonder. Inside the cramped kitchen more perspiration oozed from Mum's brow than during any of her midweek tennis games, the Metter's No.2 stove providing even greater zest to an Australian heat wave; no insulation under the rusty corrugated iron roof as reprieve either. Of course refrigeration was in its infancy, air conditioning had yet to be developed, its nearest cousin the Coolgardie safe, but only slightly cooler if you were the size of a leftover leg of lamb. The rest of us sweltered. And dripped.

Chores were allocated, albeit assiduously; the threat of withholding our threepence pocket money all that was needed to insure compliance. From recent calculations I'm still owed about 12 pounds 11 shillings and nine pence. But with compounding interest it could be much more, as Grumps, my high school economics teacher, dictated in note taking. Few passed that particular subject as both were boring.

In the midst of this chaos we progeny were commanded to make ourselves useful and set the table. This involved laying out the black tinged EPNS cutlery and the 'good' gold-lined crockery on the lace tablecloth only seen on special occasions, no risks to be taken with everyday use. For that we were to be thankful, for our outer Melburnian suburb had its own crockery maker, Johnson's. From down in Lusher Road, locally known as Slusher Road when it flooded in winter, Dad had procured plenty of cheap factory seconds. That none of them matched, or sat level, epitomised the days of post-war austerity, even our kitchen cupboard doors were also similarly mismatched in colour. These days they say contrast is fashionable but some thought then it was a post-war shortage of paint. Rationing had only just ended. Could the burden of repaying Australia's Lend-Lease war debt to America extend to us all forever, I postured.

As my mission in life was to keep up the wood for the voracious stove, this meant kindling for lighting followed by split firewood, preferably all about 1½ by 1½ inches and a foot long. Dad and I had gathered the wood from the roadside, especially after the SEC cleared the powerlines and left the wood in foot lengths for the working class like us. No one was too proud to scavenge then; these days they call it recycling but put a tax on it. Strange. However using wood as a fuel did demand planning. All the wood had to be carted home, split and stacked a year for drying beforehand. Of course, some might say these days, to reduce environmental smoke. Nah, it was because wet wood wouldn't light, burnt poorly and you needed so much more. Certainly not rocket science then, a phrase not even thought of, the moon way too far away for serious consideration.

Mum's old stove had seen better days. Somewhere a hole had deviously rusted its way through between the firebox and the oven, demanding constant attention on behalf of the cook, our portly and frayed Mum. Cakes always burnt black on that one side, the Christmas roast was no different and so required regular turning. Any which way it resulted in all sides of the roast being burnt, but no one was game to say anything as the potatoes in the tray always came out beautifully crisp more like the local fish and chip shop. Of course Mum made the gravy from the roast's juices, only having to stir a little plain flour in towards the end. In other times she saved the solidified lard for cooking, little in our household was wasted, even if we all became heart attacks waiting to happen later in life. Don't get me started on the amount of salt we ingested, no meal complete without a lavish sprinkling of high blood pressure, few relations lived beyond their Christian three score years and ten then.

Dad, being the self-appointed carver of the first water, would spend an inordinate amount of time sharpening the sole bone-handled carving knife. Much gnashing of teeth and shrill drawing of the steel until blood was just oozing as he sliced, from his thumb usually. By now the meat was generally coldish, the fat congealing and the knife considerably thinner. Mum, however, after many years of marriage, knew his idiosyncrasies well and had placed the dinner plates in the oven where at least one side of the plate grew warm. On the stove top our home grown peas were now better suited for warfare as rock hard bullets, the pumpkin represented soup, the beans withered to string and the rest of the family similar as we waited for the repast. Impatiently too, as our bone handled cutlery tapped on the table top. By this time it was past two in the afternoon and the table legs took on a particularly good look for a little gnaw. After all, the cat sharpened its claws and teeth on the legs, why not us?

Grandma's role in the meal had started at least a month beforehand with preparing the pudding. Never once referring to a recipe, she threw all the dried Mildura sultanas, raisins and shrivelled dates found in her cupboard into some Penfold's sherry for soaking. Being staunch Presbyterians meant alcohol could only be used for cooking, but also being Christian meant nothing should be wasted either, if you get my drift. No use-by dates, only Afghani then. Along with gluggy but delicious butcher's suet, Gippsland butter and lots of Queensland sugar, the pudding now resembled a gigantic mushroom, wrapped in an old threadbare pillowcase, which had been boiled for ages and hung up to cure in her fireplace. Her pudding was something that few could wish for a second helping, it entered one's stomach as a lead balloon. Adults were treated to lumpy Birds custard waved over by a brandy cork; us kids had to be content with cream, our arteries contracting as we gorged. Did I mention the cream was unpasteurised, one of Dad's Grade Six parents running a dairy herd and hoping for good marks. If we had been good, drinks included Devondale apple juice and were allowed to pour Lilydale cider for the adults. Carefully. As to whether cider was alcoholic was answered by Dad's index finger poised over lips. Another father-son conspiracy. Right.

For colour and tradition, Grandma always added her festive touch of inserting a silver coin into the pudding, but in the name of fairness, only one per dish and just before serving. Maybe she realised just how keen we all were to find the thruppence, especially when it represented a whole week's pocket money. With all of us distracted with chores she almost surgically inserted the seven coins into our servings and then revelled as we discovered our fortune a few minutes later. With much excitement, as though we never knew what she'd done, her apron blackened with polishing.

Adults recycled their winnings, something we kids were allowed to keep. One hiccup though, on Grandpa's scraped dish no sign of his silver. What! Not that he seemed to notice, or mind, after all he probably thought it was thruppence saved if she hadn't blessed his pudding.

Out of Grandpa's missing coin was born a family mystery. Where had it gone? Or had it even been inserted, after all Grandma had only gone to Grade Seven, could a miscount have occurred? However anyone knowing her would be quickly impressed by her innate intelligence, especially arithmetic and written. Not even the next door butcher dared to rest his finger on the scales when her all-seeing blue eyes were supposedly perusing the purse.

'Well?' asked Grandma.

Grandpa shrugged his already bowed shoulders. Apparently this was something that was not going to be ignored. Their weather-boarded dunny awaited outdoors, a dank cobwebbed pan service adjoining the narrow back laneway and his printing workshop. Dark as the inside of a cow even in daytime, graced by only old newspapers and a horde of insatiable mosquitoes. Hardly a convivial place for faecal exploration or olfactory sensitivity. At least we had a modern septic tank across the road, I knew how that worked along with other canals, alimentary and sewers not Suez; biology was a subject passed for once.

Days progressed. But so developed the family mystery into folklore, Grandpa's misplaced thruppence. Where was it again? When would it surface? Or sink? Exactly who would find it? Yuk! Main topic of conversation every teatime though despite being shushed.

A day or so later, our father awaited his opportunity for a wild thought. 'Any change yet Dad?'

To coin a phrase, that is.

But as in mid-breath, everyone suddenly paused. And whilst we fixated on Grandpa's downcast, but teddy-bear like brown eyes, between ink-stained fingers the shiniest sixpence we'd ever seen, magically appeared, to be greeted by a collective gasp. Sixpence? Wow!

'Obviously gained, err, some interest on its passage.'

Blame the Pink Umbrella

My view, a monochrome picture, except for one item, a type of pulsing pink star.

It seemed any Swiss train station in springtime hummed like a hive, the narrow platforms of Visp, gateway to the snow clad alps above, no exception. From my vantage point leaning over the upper level balustrade, I marvelled at the flow of humanity to and froing along a myriad of train platforms as bees out in search of blossom. The smell of hot electric motors and brakes wafted up to the unroofed Visp station as the softest of rain drizzled down.

That's when I first saw her, or should I say an undulating pink umbrella, a horde of black haired-heads closely trailing. To the tour group the upraised umbrella would have been their leader's beacon to follow, a type of pied piper, the obedient followers being led almost mindlessly along a river of shiny rail.

But something was wrong. The clustered group hesitated only momentarily before subtly changing direction alongside a second umbrella, as the new unbeknown tour leader I glimpsed, now had a ponytail of fair hair and lithe figure; the first umbrella bearer had dropped from vision to tie shoelaces. If I had blinked the change would have been missed. But what made it fascinating was that Pink Umbrella Number Two had absolutely no idea why 40 jabbering tourists now followed her every step along the platform.

She would slow, and behind they would slow; she stopped, they stopped, she turned, they turned; she ran, they ran. Once, when she stamped her foot in exasperation, a couple even mimicked, their cameras with seemingly metre-long lenses always at the ready. I could hardly restrain my mirth, the giggling making all around the balustrade wonder at the joke only I had seen.

Even when Pink Umbrella Number Two shooed them angrily away, they slowed, but crept up the instant her back turned. The first pink umbrella tour leader now frantically followed her sheep vainly bleating as she tried to break the outer cordon.

My volcanic laughter erupted. The pantomime beneath had now become a farcical contest between two pink umbrellas shaking at one another, the gabble of voices drawing me closer. That the confused tourists parted like a comb to a haircut I put down to my six foot frame towering over their heads.

'These terrorists are stalking me,' from the mêlée a light voice rose, one filled with frustration. 'Can someone tell them to go home, bloody tourists.'

'Tief! You haf stolen my grope, vat are you tryink to do?' I heard a response from the outer. 'Give zem back to me, you imposter,' the anger was tinged with Germanic accent.

'Tell them to stop following or I will call the police,' was the reply.

Confusion reigned as the horde edged even closer to Pink Umbrella Number Two, its grip on them unassailable.

'I saw it all, it was the umbrella's fault,' I yelled out to all around, 'blame the pink umbrella,' my laughter igniting a group titter. Camera flashes flashed and, as the reality hit, soon everyone was laughing. Except one.

Next second my ankle was on fire as the fiercest set of grey eyes blazed, the smile I wanted to see lost on her drawn lips, Pink Umbrella Number Two, aah! I braced myself for a second blow but the ground had suddenly risen as my world collapsed, my only sight was that of a set of shapely legs diminishing, the legs of a mule, I wondered. If there was a distinct time my sceptical heart lurched it was then. What passion, I was in awe; eyes, looks, legs clad in black tights all the way up to a cute derrière, the mini skirt hiding little. I literally fell under her spell as she scurried towards the eastern cog railway platform, the pink umbrella now furtively furled against her side. That the ground smelt as a smoker's ash tray meant nothing in my fallen trance. And if she had not glanced back through the throng and poked out her tongue at me, this story would have finished right here.

Whilst it took two days searching high and low at the end of the line in carless Zermatt, I found my assailant. Eventually. Wearing a short black apron over familiar tights, my hunch proven. Quaint café halfway down the wooden clad street; small, only ten or so tables. Old, dimly lit, but with not a cobweb in sight, I sat down. Overhead the mighty Matterhorn glittered with sun-kissed snow as if challenging me to a climbing duel to which many had succumbed, the cemetery in the next street testament. I braced myself.

'Oui?' she asked, her bewitching eyes not lifting from the pad.

'Café au lait, si vous plaît,' I said.

'Bien sûr.'

And then later, when I thought my order had been forgotten.

'Merci.'

'My pleasure, sorry for the delay.' she said, before gasping. 'Oh, it is you again, the joker, what are you doing here?'

I grinned at the memory, before grasping my ankle in reflex. 'That your pink umbrella kidnapped so many, so interesting. Should have seen your face. But you'll be pleased to know some swelling on my leg has gone down, although the doctor has not ruled out amputation.' That I chortled may not have helped.

'A pity, oh, I'm so sorry,' she replied, no apology in her eyes.

For a flash I was puzzled but then my groin caught fire as hot coffee spilled.

'Ahh!' What a temper this minx had, I thought, as my burning trousers clung relentlessly. Maybe reluctant concern resurfaced because next a finger pointed, 'The toilet is outback, past the kitchen. You can clean up there before you leave,' a half smile lingered.

After the bathroom visit, with pants still wet and clinging, an angry clash of saucepans made me glance sideways into the kitchen. Inside, layered mountains of discoloured dishes leaned as Swiss towers of Pisa, not a single portion of bench was clear. No wonder the café was free of flies, there was no space for them to land.

The chef's eyes barely lifted from his pans when I rolled my sleeves. Whether he noted my presence I couldn't be sure. Initially. But then a hand gestured towards the aprons hanging behind the door and I got to work. All this gave me an opportunity to appraise the café's workings. Three staff, waitress, chef and a missing dish washer, I surmised; only breakfast and lunch too, by the menu.

I washed, washed and washed some more. Through a square hatch the balding chef pushed full plates whilst I was expected to clear the returned dirty ones. So I scrubbed, washed and dried some more, not taking me long to realise Emile was mute, so by crude sign language I learnt lots. The cafe was managed by the waitress whilst her parents lived in southern France. Yes, the previous kitchen hand had quit, no one stayed, mainly due to the 'patronne's' quick temper. No, Selina was likely to share his unmarried fate and stay that way. He pointed to the ring finger and shook his head. Sometimes she was sad, he mimicked tears, sometimes she could be almost happy, he grimaced, but most times Selina was fussy and rapid to take offence. I would be best to behave and work hard, he shook his finger in mock admonishment. I nodded and made him a coffee; very weak, three sugars.

By late afternoon the dishes stopped coming through the hatch. Emile's pans were all hanging shiny, the kitchen looked clean and tidy. Plus I had forgotten the satisfaction of seeing a job finished well.

That was when Selina pushed open the kitchen door. Emile sensed the opportunity, raised his thumb with a grin, pushed past me and then left. This was the first time I saw her open-mouthed, almost too shocked for words, but not for long.

'It is you once more! What are you doing here?' her earlier words repeated.

'You said to clean up here, so I did,' I said, waving across the kitchen and putting on my brightest smile.

'Again you are trying to make fun of me, I think.'

'Not anymore,' I said and quickly sidled out. And if my limp suddenly worsened in front of her, so be it.

Each day following brought new but subtle changes. The second day Emile made me a special plate of titbits to peck from during my duties, on the third day a tray of leftovers for tea at my backpackers. Another day he showed me how to prepare a simple soufflé; being accepted meant more than I thought, maybe it was mutual. His silent life can't have been much fun. But the fifth day saw Selina standing in the kitchen doorway, barring my entry.

'You should not be here,' she said, 'I have not employed you.' Then she turned sideways, pointing, 'My favours cannot be bought, go.'

It was then I felt a push in the back as Emile came into view. His hands gesticulated wildly; he wrenching open the adjoining door and bowing to Selina as if to say, this is my domain, if he goes, I go. I felt strangely touched.

After that I kept heaving dishes from the hatch one tray after the other until it felt as though we had served all of Switzerland. Singlehanded. Once my fingers touched something soft, her fingers being withdrawn as if burnt.

But Friday night found an envelope next to my coat. Inside were wages, a handful of crumpled Swiss franc notes. I wrote 'Neither can I be bought' on the envelope and placed it back in the hatch. Touché.

At the end of the second week, the kitchen received another rare visit, even Emile seemed surprised. Quickly he found some tasty morsel of pan-fried marinated goat for her to sample, whilst I made coffees and put one in her hand. Very strong, dash of skinny milk, no sugar.

'The job agency is having trouble finding a kitchen hand at such short notice,' she said, her dismissive tone and floating hand suggesting I could stay under sufferance, 'maybe you could serve meals out front sometimes when we are busy.'

While Emile buried himself cooking on the stove, I nodded my head. 'The surgeon says surgery may not be necessary on my leg after all. Look, the limp is less,' I said, wondering if it was too late to feign a fall into her lap.

'Interesting,' she said, a wry grin threatening to break out, 'considering I kicked the other leg. By the way, Franz, you've just put salt into your coffee.'

At least she had learnt my name, I consoled myself.

It was now the third week.

As I lifted the rubbish bin lid, something memorable greeted my eyes; it was her pink umbrella, now discarded. Was this symbolic like my plaintive efforts, I wondered, glancing around before secreting it under my shirt. Back in my cramped room I unfurled the crumpled petals. Unless my senses had been further overtaken, the faintest of her scent remained, Beautiful by Images, our opposition. But too high on the nose, good notes but an unimaginative oval bottle; I felt my old creativeness return. Maybe I should head off to the hardware store to get some gear, now there was a reason.

The next time we 'met' in the hatch was not so fleeting. Once, during this second last week I managed to rest my hand on hers, the oddest of meetings at which she hesitated until Emile coughed behind, his next order was ready and getting cold. My back felt hot as her eyes bored.

That last Saturday I wondered what would happen next. By now my hands were permanently wrinkled like elephants' skin whilst I had given up receiving more encouraging signs from Selina, and that words we should have said to one another would remain unheard. My month's annual leave was over, my bags were packed, soon I would catch the morning's train home and return to my job far away, spurned.

By six I had the kitchen washing up under control and would have left if only Emile had finished his last spasm of cooking. It was weird as there were no orders, and, peering through the hatch, all out front was quiet too. He motioned me to sit down, even shepherding Selina from behind the till where she had been counting the week's takings. Then, as she glowered, candles were lit, a bottle popped, dishes clanked and the waft of a rich wine sauce surrounded the two of us and commandeered our senses.

Even Selina's eyes widened at the plates; Emile had pulled out all the stops, it was a meal fit for royalty.

The back door slammed, we looked at one another realising we were alone, silence reigning. I hesitated a full minute, whilst she resisted only seconds longer before I poured the champagne and paid tribute to his feast. Neither of us could ignore the enticement of sensuous food and wine.

'Selina,' I said, 'it appears words don't come easily between us, only actions,' I grinned, bending down to rub my leg. Which one was it now?

'But Franz, I know nothing about you or where you come from, although the accent sounds French,' she said, clinking her glass against mine, 'you could be a serial killer, for instance.'

'Sorry to disappoint you, mon amour, nothing so exciting, I'm afraid,' I said, laughing. 'But being French is partly true, I'm Australian but work in a Grasse perfume factory there.'

Her eyebrows rose. 'As a glass designer,' I added, 'designing bottles for perfumes.' From my pocket I pulled out the Perspex model that had occupied idle hours. In my palm rested a tiny inverted umbrella and painted pink, the handle a screw top lid, my best work so far.

Both of us drew breath, but for differing reasons.

'Keep this, Selina, it is a farewell present from me. Something unique, something to show how I feel about you.'

Maybe it was a zany idea, the pink umbrella shaped bottle, the handle as the top, maybe not. For a moment she paused, before sampling the scent of alpine flowers I had crushed inside. Her eyes fluttered, her mouth opened in apparent ecstasy, a smile flickered and I knew it was going to be a commercial success but my hopes were based closer, much closer. Would the flickering smile grow?

After that, I don't remember much. Her lips were softer than expected, but no resistance did I feel, only eagerness to kiss, and touch. Certainly no umbrella could have fitted between us, I was hers and she gave herself completely. Her upstairs flat was closer, the stairs steep and creaking, the single bed hard and narrow, neither mattered.

Nothing has changed, except the bed. For that, blame the pink umbrella.

He Says, She Says

'Hey Gabe, betcha fifty bucks you can't date that hot chick over at 10B,' my orderly mate says, his bony elbow painfully nudging ribs before whispering, 'think her name is Alicia. Twenty points for sure. Forget your blonde wet dream.' Ah Giorgio, always first on the scene to dispense care and attention, my love-life mentor whose dating stats could have set a hospital record, if only it was PC. 'Patient Care' personally dispensed with Italian charisma, he'd made his mantra, thrusting an upright fist to the sky and flexing bicycle tube biceps. Yeah, right.

Working as a hospital occupational therapist does have its moments. Like now; two, not one, babes leaning over my patient Josh, and kissing too. Simultaneously, and followed by hugging no less. What did he have I didn't? The quandary bored into my work-addled brain. Twelve hour shifts does things to reasoning. Or jealousy perhaps?

'You're on.' Not only tight jean clad hips but with eyes that could have restarted stalled hearts from ten metres and a smile that rippled across lips like spring pond breeze. But would she fancy me? Fifty dollars from Giorgio the Italian stallion would be the sweetest of all payoffs too. Hang on, was that a two fingered salute she gave Josh? Aha. My odds shifted a gear as imagination fantasised. So when she turned and smiled in my direction, something melted within me, deep down and moulded into resolve. And belief in the power of prayer. Physical attraction five points.

Amazing the effect of a white gown over my scrubs and wheelchair borrowed from the foyer too. Suddenly I was at patient level and followed, somewhat zigzagged towards the car park. Stalking? Nah.

So when a machine gun rattle started, I had my wheelchair positioned alongside within seconds, well almost. Fate ruled. That a bet is a bet overruled emotional reserve.

'Wait up, I'm Gabe, saw you in Josh's ward. Sounds like the battery,' I said, 'flip the bonnet.' Was I meant to date tonight?

'But can you, I mean, fix it? Seeing you are …'

'Nothing to a strong bronzed Aussie guy,' I said, putting my best wheel forward. Pity the left brake wasn't on as I lurched 180 degrees facing back at the entrance. Where was everyone? Whoah. Pooh happens, okay? Hang-on, was that a cough or snigger?

With the recalcitrant battery terminal hot under my fingers I could almost feel her skin against mine. So close as she leant against me, I nearly swooned. A plaintive look that suggested I'm yours if only my car starts. Would Giorgio's advice mislead me?

As I levered my Leatherman tool into the terminal, her car leapt into life. Yes! Good Samaritan, five points. Of course having a dad as a mechanic helped. Raising a thumb to the night air, and resting my other on the mudguard, I winked to Alicia. Big mistake, maybe.

Who could realise how quickly a bonnet falls. Underneath, my fingers took on a new role. Hit, miss or pretend? Bang!

'Any chance of kissing it better? Please.' my plea as if childlike.

And if I moved my fingers up to lip level, so be it. For infinite time we indulged in liplock and forgot Giorgio. OMG. If someone could transport a person to a world of sensuousness, Alicia did. Emotional connectedness, five points.

'Just been discharged for the night too,' I said, 'Taxis can be terribly unreliable and expensive.'

'So the least I can do is give you a lift home,' she said, her eyes still bulging.

'Well, only if you insist,' I said, in an instant manoeuvring the wheel chair to the passenger's doorway. Which somehow seemed to be evasive, one handed. How could anyone be disabled and play sport in these contraptions?

'Wasn't it your other hand I squashed?' she said. Gosh, I loved that quizzical smile of hers, seemed to grow on me every time.

'Sympathetic phantom pain,' I said, 'one hand sympathises with the other, common problem with nerve damage victims.'

Her eyes drilled for signs of madness. 'Although on second thoughts, you could be a serial killer.'

'In a wheelchair? Anyway I'm more of a toast man myself,' I said, her answer a tickling giggle.

We left.

'Could you pull over here?' I said, the 'mick' church looming alongside next to the red light. 'Maybe a moment of reflection might help in our hours of need.' And just maybe her gold chained cross could be exploited further, I thought. Not the faintest of velvet-lined cleavage, although the thought of soft touch had flitted between my neurons.

'Now if we hold hands here in front of the altar, maybe our prayers might be answered.' There I took my time only glancing sideways on 98, 99, 100. No reaction, so I repeated my mother's prayer, or what I could recall. It had always been muttered under breath, especially when Dad came home late.

'Hail or rain, don't ever race. Blessed is he who cleans up their room, oh dear Jesus. Holy Connolly, preface cinders, now to earth, ah, men.'

As if on cue I groaned, shook my frame and began to flex cramped legs. Isn't that how faith works? Leaning forward as an invalid I took my first faltering steps, she wide-eyed in sympathy, the expression on Alicia's face one of wonder. Or was it mirth, no matter. When I staggered, how quickly she was at my side, her smile broader than a river, which made my blood run as fast.

'It's a miracle! How hard I have prayed, maybe it takes the power of two, Alicia.' Miracles surely rated the missing five points. 'Though I'm a bit broke at present, I think we should celebrate; would you go out with me on a date? Whadayasay?'

Maybe the deepest of thought crossed her sun-kissed face. 'How do you know my name?' she said.

And smiled.

She says:
Can't believe the day I've just had.

Deep depths, thoughtful plateau, then laughs. Life.

A guy, reasonably cute, but oh-so obvious even to the blind society, came onto me. Gabe. Not that I minded for once, my last ex was a dickhead only after one thing. As if.

Who would have doubted how my bro got his back broke? By an axe murderer or on his wretched trail bike? Certainly not me. Or by a jealous husband catching him in the act, yes, possibly more likely! Always wheeling and dealing. Cracked C3 vertebra supposedly fixable though. So this day saw his latest squeeze and me visiting in hospital. Claustrophobic place reeking of disinfectant and piped music, no matter how good the ventilation; spinal rehab always sent my brain into overdrive. Why are guys such risk takers and play actors? Surely not for our attention. And why was the world full of misguided matchmakers?

Then pooh happened on leaving, as it does; my beloved Fiat Cinquecento wouldn't start, only farted in staccato fashion, then nothing. Latin appearance over reliability, typical. More cantankerous than any Italian male and picking its moments as precisely to exert max influence.

So a wheelchair guy had followed me out, either to perve on my undies as I got in or whatever. No matter, he exerts some form of magic and gets the Turin machine started. Couldn't be so bad after-all. How dangerous could he be in a wheelchair? With alluring facial features that could have sold aftershave, I wondered.

But then I dropped the bonnet on his fingers. Oh bugger! Like a kid wanted me to kiss it better. What harm in that? So as we smooched his finger lips got in the way; it was then I realised interesting territory lay ahead. Great lips, soft, all encompassing technique and warm, didn't close his eyes either. Not only was Gabe a brilliant kisser or perhaps opportunistic womaniser; why did no one warn me, did I care, hmm.

'A miracle it truly seems. But there's something about you I can't quite put my finger on,' I said.

'That'll be my sore hand, Alicia. So I think we should celebrate,' Gabe said, clutching me with purposeful hands more suited to massage, but now still wobbling.

'This is all happening very fast,' I said. 'And you're not like anyone I've met before.'

He laughed with his eyes, 'That's because we haven't met before,' he said. 'Would you go out with me on a date? Whadayasay?'

Of course Josh had told me about his physio, Gabe. 'Unlucky in love,' he said. 'Join the queue,' I answered. 'Think you'd be a good match, funny guy.' As if, what would my brother know? My life needed no complications. Who needed love anyway? Then as Gabe leaned somewhat against me, I wondered. Warmth, love, security? What a wooer.

'First kiss me again, a little slower though, and then we'll see,' I said, a smile escaping to this crazy guy. 'Of course it can't be an upmarket date, I could only lend Josh $50.'

About the Author

Unashamedly a baby boomer, John was born in Melbourne, Victoria in 1950 and has lived in Western Australia since 1974. Originally trained as a motor mechanic, he was 'driven' into TAFE teaching, gained a university education degree in media/language (a 'degree of insanity', in John's words) and has written educational resources. All this whilst trying to train 30 years worth of apprentices how to fix things without breaking them. At the height of his teaching career he trained TAFE teachers around WA. Still in love with his wife Elizabeth, over 41 years, they have 3 children and 2 grandchildren across Perth and overseas. Come home, he pleads, all is forgiven, well just not yet. I promise not to tell any more 'Dad' jokes! Well, except in my Op Shop. Beware!

Wine by the Glass

'All people want to know they are loved and are not alone,'

Accident and Emergency nurse, 2013.

This book is dedicated to all my family and friends. My life has been an inspiring journey with many crossroads, steep hills, breathtaking summits and meandering valleys along the way, albeit so far. Anyway you know who you are … I hope.

But writers are carers and generous sharers. Heartfelt thanks go for the inspiring workshops of:

Hazel Edwards
Stephanie Holt
Anna Jacobs
Lee Kofman
Candice Lemon-Scott
Juliet Marillier
Susan Midalia
Meg Mundell
Sonia Orchard

Here my life-support team should also be named for posterity, thanked and attributed for any possible blame.

My ever loving wife Elizabeth and family, Craig, Kirsty, and Bryn. My grandchildren Eleni and Clem. My writing/editing mentor, Candice Lemon–Scott, cover artist/friend Ronnie Brincat and cover model Deema Brincat. Writers Victoria. Busybird Publishing team.

Congratulations, you've bought an award-winning book. Literally!

Its current credentials are:

- *Grandma's Maid, Mary* won the 2011 Fellowship of Australian Writers Memoir Award and was also published in the 2012 Spring Fast Fiction magazine

- *Eileen's Story* won Second Prize in the 2012 Scribes Writers Short Story Competition

- *Collaborative Consumption* was Shortlisted in the 2012 Positive Words Short Story Competition

- *Open Wide* was Shortlisted in the 2011 Fellowship of Australian Writers, Angelo B. Natoli Short Story Award

- *Maybe, Maybe Not* was Commended by Scribes Writers for their 2011 Short Story Award

- *How to Write a book in 10 weeks* won a Commendation in the 2011 Fellowship of Australian Writers, Lyndall Hadow/Donald Stuart Short Story Award

- *The legendary Bulldust Bill* won a Commendation in the 2015 Best of Times competition and was Long-listed in the 2012 Alan Marshall Short Story Award

- *Duel Control* was awarded publication in the 2013 Short and Twisted Collection

- *When Dad kicked the bucket* won Second prize and publication in the 2014 Positive Words Short Story Competition

- *A fair deal* won First Prize in the 2015 Henry Lawson Society Short Story Awards

- *To coin a phrase* achieved a Commendation and was e-published in the humorous 2015 Best of Times collection

- *Dog, man's worst fiend* was Highly Commended in the 2016 Stringybark Short Stories and published in 'Standing By'

- *Blame the pink umbrella* was Shortlisted in the 2016 Bundaberg Writers Club Short Story competition

- *Wine by the glass* book project was short listed in 2016 by Busybird Publishing and provided the impetus for this publication

- *He says, she says* was awarded publication in the 2017 Short and Twisted Competition

And so on ...

Notes on the Stories by the Author

1. **Grandma's Maid, Mary.** For most people an all encompassing realisation is that family is by far the greatest influence on their life. Thus it was for me. Our Grandma had a maid, didn't everyone? And with Mary having such a profound influence on us kids, who could be left without lifetime manners and consideration for others?

2. **How to Write a Book (in 10 Weeks).** This tale was inspired by my elder sister, a university lecturer, who made me ponder the modern dilemma of on-line learning and its issues. Combined with modern emotional tensions how will we all romance one another in future? With local dances a thing of the past, who really is who? How do we meet in reality that one-in-a-million person who will make our heart spin at a million-miles-an-hour?

Alicia is a modern, independent young lady, feisty, committed and with a need to be wanted. Some facts cannot be disputed, she's a caring kindergarten teacher and she loves her grandmother. She also owns a handy laptop computer. Gran is experiencing difficulties at the other end of her life and wants to record her story of love before it's too late. Could she inspire Alicia to find her own reason to love? Enter Alistair, a moonlighting high school teacher masquerading as Gran's U3A teacher who promises to fulfil her last desire in the writing class. Follow a brief excursion into their lives.

3. **Open Wide.** Having grown up associating the harrowing visit with pain and misery, let alone cost, I marvel at today's dentistry where power and patient are somewhat more evenly balanced. Just as it should be. How does a younger person like Aleisha deal with Gene her dentist, I wonder? Especially when he perceives her recently-arrived status and decides to provide advice on the Australian way of life.

4. **Maybe, Maybe Not.** Some long years ago out of the window of a Contiki bus I witnessed the near gang-rape of a fellow young Australian traveller at a Turkey border. The outrage and shame of being a man has never left me and hope it will persuade others to consider their travel options more carefully. When Josh 'buys' the release of a white slave from a drug-addled existence it leaves Alyssa always in his debt. Why her, why had he risked his life and how can she ever repay him?

5. **Collaborative Consumption**. Using stuff we already have to get the stuff we want – all without accumulating more stuff. For me, I love the sheer randomness of life, how we can meet someone so attractive and titillating one minute and yet another so repulsive the next. Fate? Or coincidence? What stuff do Sam and Kieran really have in common to share?

6. **The Legendary Bulldust Bill.** Here my mechanic's background has me marvelling at the eccentric characters that permeate each trade. But for the reader I ask them to differentiate the personality from their proficiency. Maybe it's alright to be eccentric. Who me? Maybe there's more to old Bulldust Bill than you think! Can bulldust baffle brains? Yup!

7. **Dog, a Man's Worst Fiend.** For most a canine companion is a source of great comfort. In our family however this was a time of great conflict, when parental expectations met the dulled reactions of sleep deprivation. Yawn and you'll miss the action! Bang, did that wake you? A man's best friend, as if!

8. **Caught Out, Court In.** This tale explores two diverse characters whose life agendas clash from the very beginning. When a crime is allegedly committed should you intervene or just ring for the police? When Graham unexpectedly returns home he catches Alicia wearing his mother's diamonds in a darkened house. Can he rehabilitate a thief and negotiate an outcome satisfactory to all?

9. **Katherine with a K.** One of my favourite characters, Katherine's feminism burns with a flame a metre high until she finally meets her match. Does something else inside finally ignite? Play along in a real game of mind-chess when she pits herself against a mystery opponent who not only can get inside her office undetected but also her head. (Sorry about the inflamed puns.)

10. **How to Have the Ideal Family.** This question has puzzled many parents from Anglo-Saxon ancestry when faced with a family union of Latin background. Of what use to the family is the potential member? Suddenly social status confronts the usefulness of Andrew, the local but ambitious plod. What male attributes could possibly win the Grilli's family approval and Angela's heart?

11. **A Sorrento Tradie and a Ring Top.** OK, as a mechanic I admit to being biased with tradies: comes from being from a family where academia ruled supreme, so the tale takes on an air of realism. Detesting pretentious snobbishness, I leave it to the reader whether true love can prevail between tradie Evan and privately schooled Amanda, or not. How can Tech ever compete with uni? How does working class prevail against old money?

12. **A Cure for Writer's Block.** Most writers experience a hiatus of thought at one time or another just as some forget just why they opened the fridge door. This tale explores the interaction of two people interacting without realising just how love can interact! How else can you explain Sophie asking Pieter, her next door neighbour, help clear her writer's block only to find Ben the district nurse intervening. Maybe she could have been interested if only Ben hadn't possessed a hidden past. Would her own weakness impede or cement an unlikely relationship?

13. **Bayerische Motoren Werke.** This tale is a conglomeration of snippets from my automotive career where the repair workshop was a hot bed of blood, sweat and emotion, a microcosm of life, I guess. Despite many people's expectations a mechanic's job is noisy, dirty and not well paid. It can, however, be very rewarding, sometimes.

In this tale please meet Ms Chewing Gum, her father, Mr Gaping Pyjamas, eves dropper, Ms Microphone and our hero Mr Mechanic. With his wayward tongue denying any chance of winning 'Employee of the Month at the dealership, can Brett perform the diagnosis of the century, get his job back and win the customer's heart?

14. **The Auction.** After the 'honeymoon' period of a relationship, couples do not always appreciate each other quite as much. This tale epitomises life and love when reality confronts imagination. Just how much is a loving partner worth in cold hard cash? Follow an auctioneer as he frantically bids for 'a not to be forgotten mystery evening with an insatiable lover.' Was his girlfriend Naomi a part-time hooker? Oh no, could marriage ever be considered a cheaper option?

15. **Sex and Drugs.** Who has not misunderstood someone else, or their actions, please stand up. OK, sit down. Is the glass half full or half empty? Would I like the person if they only just ... or should I just follow my innermost instincts? Should Alison trust a drug-dealing tenant and should Jamie trust a hooker-cum tenant? Then what about Albert, the child Alison claims as her own, but isn't. Confused? Unravel the tangle.

16. **My Dad, the Greenie.** Teenagers usually place their parents somewhere between a pedestal and the grave. In this tale the kid's favourite dad attempts to make his family the suburb's most environmentally friendly. Will Dad achieve the family accolades that he seeks and save their world singlehanded?

17. **Transumerism.** This modern marketing concept was courtesy of a Virgin flight magazine. Who says you can't learn something from every mile-high journey? Tegan was convinced she needed to only hire an evening escort until she met Emile, or was it Marcel? So why buy when you can hire without all the attendant risks of ownership? Unless you really want a life membership, of course.

18. **Not What it Seems.** With all of us vulnerable to life's forces at one stage or another, these two people are forced together by circumstances greater than themselves. Desperately trying to clear himself, Max realises his future lies with finding an elusive workmate Mikael, or at least that what it seems.

19. **What about Emily's Father?** Too often a man's adolescent and strongest emotions are held captive without release, something to be unravelled in later life. When Thomas, now in his 30's, is charmed by his childhood sweetheart's child, Emily, what will be the outcome with her mother? Could Bugs Bunny bring them all together after so long? But then, what about Emily's father?

20. **Eileen's Story.** Aren't we but mainly a product of our genes? Without our imaginative Grandma, how could we all seven of us be seated equally at the round family table? And whilst Eileen, with her wonky leg holding court at the head at the table, could anyone question who was the true matriarch cum chairperson?

21. **Caution, Duel Control.** A work colleague inadvertently gave me the idea for this story based on his son meeting his true love over the Internet. Marie enlists the guidance of an Internet dating service to meet Trent, a high level professional with twin alternating responsibilities. How can she fault an executive in an environmental recycling position as a well as on a steering committee? Then when Heinz, the local bin-foraging dog intervenes, driving Marie to rubbish rage, what will be the outcome?

22. **When Dad Kicked the Bucket.** Most families possess at least one unique cringe-worthy circumstance that defines to whom they belong. Then we leave home only to discover how hard it really is to lead perfect lives. Maybe that is what makes

finally appreciate our own family and embrace it warts and all. How similar is this family of mine to yours?

23. **A Fair Deal.** Do all children have to have both parents? In this modern world more and more families are split. Here father and son Piers are doing just fine by themselves all based on a world of negotiated trust and honesty. But is this the essential truth? Maybe life is not always fair.

24. **To Coin a Phrase.** Whilst Christmas time for some can be a time of great tension when many are gathered in a space for few, ours weren't. Take a trip down memory lane and my grandfather's alimentary canal, to coin a phrase, that is.

25. **Blame the Pink Umbrella.** For those who experience group travel overseas, this tale may be familiar as you blindly follow your leader's staff held high through foreign streets. Here a misunderstanding has Franz following his heart to Selina instead of his train ticket. Knowing 'faint heart won't win fair maiden' literally drives him to new heights but to no avail. Give up or try harder? Just when should unrequited love be relinquished? Or not, hmm.

26. **He Says, She Says.** Here we see a casual encounter through two differing sets of eyes. Will a bet motivate wheelchair-bound Gabe to date hospital visitor Alicia?